Praise for *Vamped*

"*Vamped* is a total delight! Diver delivers a delightful cast of undead characters and a fresh, fast take on the vampire mythos. Next installment, please!"

—Rachel Caine, *New York Times* bestselling author of the Morganville Vampires series

"I really sank my teeth into Lucienne Diver's *Vamped*. A fun, frothy teenage romp with lots of action, a little shopping, and a cute vampire guy. Who could ask for more?"

—Marley Gibson, author of *Ghost Huntress: The Awakening*

"This book rollicked along, full of humor, romance, and action. Gina is a smart-aleck heroine worth reading about, a sort of teenage Betsy Taylor (*Undead and Unwed*) with a lot of Cher Horowitz ("Clueless") thrown in. Fans of Katie Maxwell will devour *Vamped*."

—Rosemary Clement-Moore, author of *Prom Dates from Hell*

"Move over, Buffy! Lucienne Diver transfuses some fresh blood into the vampire genre. Feisty, fashionable, and fun— *Vamped* is a story readers will sink their teeth into and finish thirsty for more."

—Mari Mancusi, author of The Blood Coven Vampires series

ReVamped

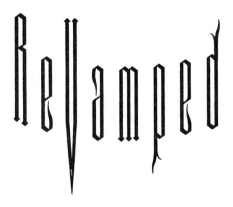

ReVamped

LUCIENNE DIVER

flux™
Woodbury, Minnesota

First Edition
First Printing, 2010

Back cover image © iStockphoto.com/Katarzyna Krawiec
Book design by Steffani Sawyer
Cover design by Lisa Novak
Front cover image © 81a/PunchStock

Flux, an imprint of Llewellyn Worldwide Ltd.

Library of Congress Cataloging-in-Publication Data
Diver, Lucienne, 1971–
  ReVamped / Lucienne Diver.—1st ed.
    p. cm.
  Summary: Gina and her boyfriend Bobby, both undead and working as spies for the government, are sent to infiltrate a high school in New York state where unexplained phenomena are causing problems, but Gina is unhappy with her cover story as an emancipated minor Goth girl.
  ISBN 978-0-7387-2129-3 (alk. paper)
  [1. Vampires—Fiction. 2. Spies—Fiction. 3. Goth culture (Subculture)—Fiction. 4. High schools—Fiction. 5. Schools—Fiction. 6. New York (State)—Fiction.] I. Title.
  PZ7.D6314Re 2010
  [Fic]—dc22
                          2010015070

Flux
Llewellyn Worldwide Ltd.
2143 Wooddale Drive
Woodbury, MN 55125-2989, U.S.A.
www.fluxnow.com

Printed in the United States of America

This one is for M'ie and T-Bird.
Love you, girls.

Quick recap: When we last left our heroine, which would be me, she and her minions—screw it, *me* and *my* minions—had just defeated a vampy vixen, a psycho-psychic, and the vampire council of Mozulla, Ohio. Go, us! There were network news vans and the whole nine yards. Unfortunately, we don't show up on film in all our fanged fabulosity, so the Feds were able to come in, sweep it all under the rug, and put us to work for them. Whether we liked it or not. Let me tell you, that just *bites*.

Now that you're up to speed, I present to you:

Gina's Rules for Surviving Super Spy School Training

1. First, the dirt and sweat and all are just too horrible to contemplate. Your sanity pretty much depends on finding your own Zen kind of happy place, like the Victoria's Secret one-day sale or poolside with your own personal cabana boy, whichever you prefer.

2. Unless you enjoy cold showers, be the first one to the bathroom in the morning, even or especially if it means body-checking your archnemesis on the way. She'll heal.

3. Cargo pants make you look hip-py. Unfortunately, the Feds have no sense of humor when it comes to giving your fatigues a miracle makeover. Tying your blouse into a belly shirt, or turning your khakis into cut-offs and making hairbands out of the remaining fabric, it turns out, are practically punishable by death.

4. If you break a nail during super spy school training, you're actually encouraged to stop and pick it up. Maybe you can do a patch job later. What you *don't* want is to leave anything behind that can later be used for some kind of forensic analysis or locator spell.

5. Making out on missions, unless it's part of your cover, is totally grounds for extra push-ups. Great for your bod, but hell on your love life.

6. When going goth—and I mean *hello,* can I get a color palette here, please?—you've totally got to strike words like totally, awesome, phat, and fresh from your vocabulary. Also, exclamation points. *Whatever,* however, is a total keeper.

7. When they're teaching lock-picking and all, hold something back. If they know just how good you are, you're going to have a really hard time sneaking out for pre-mission snogging with your honey.

8. Who are "they," you ask? I could tell you, but then I'd have to kill you. And trust me, no one would

ever find the body. 'Course that might be because you'd become one of us—the few, the proud, the unmentionables, and I'm not talking about those Vicky's Secret panties here, people.

1

I sat in the middle of spook central's briefing room, staring at the sorry state of my manicure rather than the blah-brown walls. Actually, *brown* was giving them too much credit. These walls didn't have enough balls for brown or bleach for what the hoity-toity might call ecru, but I just call *bor*ing. They'd sort of curled up and died somewhere in between. There weren't even any motivational posters to break up the color block. Only a bunch of high-tech AV equipment. My boyfriend, Bobby, had about geeked out the first time he'd seen it. Although, calling Bobby "geeked out" was like saying the sun was shiny or water wet. Kinda redundant and repetitive.

I sat between Bobby and Rick-the-rat, a rose between two thorns. I was contemplating a mani-pedi in fuchsia or cobalt or something to liven up the place—and me—when it registered on me what Agent Stuffed Shirt had just said.

"Come again?" I asked, sure I'd heard wrong, even with all my undead enhancements like super-hearing and Spidey-senses.

"You'll be going undercover as a goth girl."

My eyes must have bugged out, as unattractive as that was. "Unh-uh. No way. I look ghostly in black!"

Agent Stick-up-her-butt, a.k.a. Stuffed Shirt's partner Maya, gave me a meaningful look over her teeny-tiny librarian glasses.

"*Even more* than usual," I added.

When I'd lived and breathed, I'd been almost religious about maintaining a certain level of tan to keep myself—at five foot nothing—from looking any more waifish than necessary. My three-inch heels never hurt either. But death has a funny way of screwing with the best-laid plans, and every day since I'd clawed my way out of the grave I could feel myself fading until I was all china-doll pale, my porcelain skin a total contrast with my long dark locks. A monochromatic wardrobe would wash me out like hotel sheets.

"Oh, I didn't realize you didn't like dark colors," said Agent Stuffed. "Let's see what else we have." He flipped through the file in front of him. "I'm so sorry, the position of pretty, pretty princess has already been filled." I recognized sarcasm when I heard it. Agent Stuff... Sid... was better than average at dishing it out. But then, so was I.

"Do you have something in a prima ballerina?" I asked. "I hear tutus are very slimming."

Bobby leaned over as if to talk sense into me, but Sid just laughed.

"I'll see what we can do for next time. For now—"

"Suck it up and deal," Rick finished for him. I gave him the stink eye. Rick was supposed to be *my* minion, not the Feds', whatever they might think. Blood was, after all, thicker than blackmail. And in vamp terms, Rick was my blood, or would be as soon as he crossed over from the land of the living. We'd done the whole blood exchange thing when he'd needed a transfusion so badly a few months back. So, I'd be his, like, dam, weird as all that was. If I was going to suffer magical motherhood at the tender age of seventeen, he owed me a whole lot more than some popsicle art and a punk attitude... something like eternal devotion.

"Children, sit," Sid commanded, before I could think of an appropriate put-down.

Bobby gave my hand a squeeze, as if *that* would stop me from running off at the mouth, but I subsided, excited despite myself to hear about our first assignment. At the very least, it would get us out of a government compound so secluded it made Area 51 look like a tourist attraction. There was nothing but scrub brush all around our gated perimeter and not a decent mochachino to be found anywhere. I couldn't drink them anymore, of course, but I could smell and remember.

Maya dimmed the lights and pressed a button that could have been anything from a detonation device to a game-show clicker, but turned out to work the movie screen in front of us. At that moment it was showing a street lined with antique-looking streetlights and brick buildings, ending at one that looked particularly historic with a mill wheel out the back, by which I guessed there was a stream there as well.

"Wappingers Falls," she began. "A quiet town on the Hudson River with a confluence of creeks and small tributaries…and ley lines." Bobby was poised to take notes, making me wonder if there'd be a quiz later and what the hell "confluence" meant anyway. Affluence I got, but confluence? The opposite, maybe. Like really terrible poverty? So sad.

"Massive dips and surges in the energy of the ley lines have been messing with our operations in the region," Maya continued. "The problem seems to be centered *here*." She clicked over to a high school pretty much like any other—brick with mirrored windows, L-shaped, looking just as squat and institutional as possible. "Maureen Benson High. Further investigation has revealed other abnormalities—falling test scores and attendance, students sleepwalking through school, sudden outbreaks of violence. You're going undercover there." She nodded toward the folders in front of us. "If you'll flip open your files, we can continue."

She paused to let everyone do her bidding, but I took my time. In a matter of months, I'd gone from the top of the high school heap to the bottom of the black ops barrel. I mean, *go goth*? What kind of assignment was that? After rescuing my classmates from the evil wench who'd turned them into her very own undead army, you'd think I'd deserve a medal at the very least, if not a tickertape parade and my own made-for-TV movie. But oh no. The Feds had made me and my minions an offer we couldn't refuse. The others had already been given field assignments. They must have saved the best for last.

"Rick, Bobby, you'll be brothers," Sid continued, bringing me back to the briefing. "Fraternal twins, actually. That will explain your simultaneous enrollment at Maureen Benson High. Maya and I will be posing as your parents. We've kept your identities pretty close to reality. The test scores are falling most notably among the "brains." Bobby'll fit right in. Rick, most of the aggression is coming, not surprisingly, from the jocks and the coaches. We'll put you on that. We'd like you to figure out what's sparking the strangeness. Is someone messing with powers they shouldn't be to assure top placement, either academic or athletic? If so, why is the weirdness leaking out to other groups?"

Bobby's blue eyes shone with the light of a thousand suns. Before the whole vamp makeover, they'd been hidden away behind Coke-bottle lenses. Now…well, they were pretty heart-stopping. Coupled with his shaggy chestnut hair, they made him look almost like the guy from *High School Musical*. And, it turned out, he had some really wicked powers, practically as off-the-charts as his IQ. Telepathy, a little bit of mind control, some telekinesis thrown in for good measure. Yup, I knew how to pick 'em.

"Gina," Sid snapped. I sat straighter and pretended I hadn't been mooning over a guy—my own, no less. "You'll be an emancipated minor. No parents in the picture and a place of your own. As I mentioned, you'll be infiltrating the goths. The arcane is right up their alley, and if anyone is tapping into the ley lines…"

… *I was to become their new BFF.*

2

I nearly balked when I saw the governmentally supplied apartment I'd been given as goth-girl Geneva Belfry. It reminded me of a postage stamp, and not the large commemorative kind either. My sink and shower were so close that I could brush my teeth and wash my hair at the same time. I guess undercover operatives posing as goth girls who'd divorced their parents didn't exactly rate penthouse suites. But still, did it have to smell like feet?

At least it was stocked to the gills with the elixir of life—blood. The real thing, brown-bottled for my convenience. It was a far cry from the rush of drinking straight from the vein, but had the advantage of the Feds' super-secret supplements. The blood was apparently infused with a sort of sunscreen potion that would allow us to stay awake during the day and even face brief bouts of sunlight, but for all we knew, it could be laced with tracers to help them track us or some kind of nanobots that could kill us remotely if we disobeyed orders. That wasn't me but Bobby talking, when they'd first briefed us on the blood. Personally, I figured that if the government wanted to get to us, they would, one way or another. I wasn't going to sweat it. I had bigger things to worry about, like what the hell I was going to wear. Because you never get a second chance to make a first impression.

I used to plan for the first day of school weeks in advance. My besties Becca and Marcy and I would put in hours of power-shopping and coordinating outfits, giving each other facials, manicures … the works. But Becca had been left behind in Ohio with the rest of the living, if you could call it that, and Marcy was off on a mission of her own. So, I was facing a new school all by myself with no one to play mirror for me, which barely mattered, really, because my wardrobe looked like something out of an old black-and-white horror film. There wasn't a single gem-tone, sparkle, or spangle in the whole batch of government-issued threads.

After discarding a dozen outfits, I finally chose a baby doll T-shirt that at least had some form to it and expressed exactly the way I was feeling: *Bite Me.* The "i" in "Bite" was dripping blood. I paired it with a pleated skirt that wasn't too hideous and a pair of fishnet stockings and examined my shoe selection. I nearly called the whole thing off right there—sneakers with flaming skulls, matte black high-tops, combat boots, platform Mary Janes. That they even *made* platform Mary Janes was a travesty of epic proportions.

I tried to think of the mission. Fashion faux pas were a small price to pay ... right? I mean, I'd gone so far as flats when we went up against the vampire council, like, a lifetime ago. And no one had died ... at least not due to the sorry state of my shoes.

Besides, with all the weirdness at school, probably no one would even notice what I wore. And at least my hair was already naturally black, so I didn't have to put up with a bad dye-job to match my new secret self. I pulled my hair into two even ponytails like the goth girl from *NCIS*, who I was using as a model since she was kind of cool, if way too perky to live.

Makeup was going to be a problem. Before we were split up following training, Marcy and I had practiced putting makeup on ourselves, using each other for feedback. I'd gotten decent marks on eyeliner and lipstick, but mascara was a lost cause. Despite their advances, even the Feds couldn't quite figure out why vamps didn't have reflections, or find a way to reverse the effect. "It's magic" didn't satisfy even the people whose undercover ops involved remote viewing research, psychic phenomena, and the under-dead.

Anyway, I figured it shouldn't be a problem unless lurking in ladies' rooms became a big part of my job description.

Cringing as I did it, I strapped on the platform Mary Janes and tried to own the look and my new name. *Geneva Belfry*, world-weary super goth, been there, done that, didn't bother to buy the T-shirt. Piece of cake. Devil's food.

I grabbed my death's head backpack, basic black of course, left the apartment with its thrift-store furniture and funny smell, and started on my way to school in my governmentally supplied wheels, a white-and-primer-colored Nissan with a gazillion miles on it and a *Dracula Is My Co-Pilot* bumper sticker. If Agents Stick and Stuffed had a sense of humor between them, I'd have thought they were kidding, but I didn't think they were big into irony.

The Feds had already transmitted their forged records to my new school, which I'd learned was, like, two hours from a city with actual culture—Saks Fifth Avenue, Lord & Taylor, *Tiffany's*. Who even knew that there was a whole state outside of New York City? Or that vast stretches of it were Edward Scissorhands suburbia or even, get this, farm and horse country. Wappingers Falls' big claim to fame, Bobby'd told me with glee, was that it was mentioned in some *Law and Order* episodes as a place where suspects or their families lived. As claims to fame went, that was almost as lame as *Washington Slept Here*. I mean, if he'd done something really exciting, maybe, but sleep? I did it all the time. No one had ever put up a plaque.

Anyway, the main office of Maureen Benson High was located just off the entrance on the short side of the L. It took a moment for the woman behind the counter to stop chatting with a coworker and take my name. Her shockingly red head bobbed up and down as she examined me.

"Bite me?" she asked, looking pointedly at my shirt.

"No thanks," I answered, "I've already eaten."

"Tastes like chicken," a voice behind me added, thick with masculine amusement.

I turned to see a guy also dressed in basic black—jeans, T-shirt, and combat boots—and wearing more chains than a bike rack. He had one piercing through his right brow, a thick chrome bar, and five more piercings marching up his left ear, and he was totally wicked hot. Instead of the blue eyes that were my usual weakness, his were a dark and intense brown to go with his dark brows and the out-of-control hair that half fell into his eyes. I wanted to run my fingers through it—just to test the thickness, of course, but that sort of thing tended to give guys ideas.

"Hey," I said instead, loading it with just the right amount of *come here often?* to keep him interested. After all, I needed to start making friends ... or at least contacts. Maybe even minions.

"Hey, yourself. You new?" Goth Guy asked.

The administration lady gave him the same hairy eyeball she was giving me, but went off in a huff when he refused to react.

"New to you," I answered.

He smiled, slow and lazy and stunning. "Ulric," he said, extending a hand.

The lady returned and handed over a form, which Goth

Guy—Ulric—grabbed out of her hand before I could. I noticed his nails matched mine, matte black, but that wasn't bonding enough to keep me from ripping my schedule back from him.

"There something you need, Toby?" the administration lady asked, a bite to her tone. I don't think she was defending me so much as hoping she could clear her office of both of us at once.

He colored up until he matched the fake blood dripping down my shirt. "No one calls me that," he answered through clenched teeth.

"Yes, they do," she said, the homeroom bell punctuating her comment.

I did my best to pretend that I was totally absorbed in my schedule and not paying them any attention, and I absolutely did not let a smile flicker across my face.

"Anyway," he said with a sneer, "I'm just here to meet the new blood. Saw you through the window," he added to me in a whisper, with a shrug toward the Plexiglas office walls.

Administration lady huffed. "Well, as long as you're here, you can show Geneva around."

"You'll write me a pass?" he asked.

"Is that what you were really after, Mr. Erickson?"

He shrugged, but she wasn't really waiting for an answer and had already started writing a million miles a minute. She tore a pink sheet off something that looked like a doctor's pad and handed it over to Ulric, who took it with one hand, took my arm with the other, and marched us out of there.

I shook off his hand outside the office and glared at him. Apparently he had enough ideas of his own, without help from me. Rarely a good thing—guys thinking for themselves.

"So, *Geneva*, eh? For real?" he asked, ignoring my death-ray glare, which, sadly, had no effect. My powers just didn't roll that way. Stupid powers.

I sighed, but I figured he got that a lot. "For real. My parents named me after the place I was conceived."

"Classy," Ulric said, pushing hair out of his eyes.

It seemed a perfect lead-in to my cover story. "Yeah, just one of my many grievances against them." *Grievances*—I'd learned that word straight out of the portfolio. My parents, the real ones, would be so proud. You know, if I weren't dead to them and all.

"At least you got a cool name out of it."

Whatever weirdness was going on in the school, Ulric sure didn't seem affected. Not that I really knew him or anything, but so far he didn't reek of mind control or zombification.

"So, you just moved here with your folks?" he asked.

"Yes and no," I answered, distracted by the sight of Bobby and Rick being led around by a swimsuit-model type with a perky little ponytail and scarlet sheath dress I'd vault sales racks to possess. In short, she was a bleached blond version of me, pre-vamping. If Bobby saw me at all, he gave no sign of it. Even though I knew he was probably just playing up his cover identity, it killed me to see him watching that hypnotic little ponytail bobbing as the Prissy Princess led the way. After all, I already knew she was his type. What if our assignment dragged on and he got bored of not being able to be with me and—

"You know them?" Ulric asked.

I must have been staring. *Wow,* I thought to myself, *way to be subtle.*

I recovered quickly. "No. Just wondering how many flies she's swatted with that tail."

"Who, Hailee? Couldn't say. She's always got so many buzzing around her."

I made a face.

"My thoughts exactly. So, what amazing sights do you want to see? The gym? The library? The place where we all hang out for smokes between classes?" he asked.

"No, no, and yes."

Here's the thing—I didn't smoke. It colors your teeth and makes your clothes stink, totally negating the positive effects of scented body wash, but it wasn't like I was going to die of lung cancer or anything if I did. By nature, I didn't even have to inhale. If I needed to light up to be in with the in crowd, I could take it.

Ulric led me through the long arm of the L toward a door halfway down that was propped open—and probably shouldn't have been—by a piece of cardboard. I patted myself on the back for learning already that the school was a long way from being secure. He didn't even look around stealthily before pushing straight through, which was either smart, since they taught us in super spy school to always look like you had every right to be exactly where you were since it put people off their game, *or* incredibly stupid, because by being smart he raised my suspicions. I could only almost follow my logic myself. I could just see myself trying to explain it to Agent Stick-up-her-butt.

I'd call suspicion an occupational hazard, but I'd always had a strict guilty-until-proven-innocent policy of my own. Especially with guys. Especially after my very *ex*-boyfriend Chaz slammed my side of his car into a tree on prom night, leading to the whole death trip. It also didn't help that my current boy toy, Bobby, hadn't told me when we hooked up that he had a communicable blood disease—as in the need to drink it on a regular basis. Not that it had worked out too badly for me really.

Just outside the propped door was a rock garden nestled where the two wings of the school joined. Or a boulder garden, more like. Bright flowers had been planted around the stones, but they were struggling to hold their own. They looked like they'd been trampled a time or two. On the largest boulder sat a single figure with her back toward us. Not smoking. I could tell because (a) no smoke—kind of a dead giveaway—and (b) she was singing. Hard to do both at the same time.

The girl's voice was haunting, and for a second she seemed to be a siren, sitting on a dangerous outcropping of rock, singing sailors to their doom. Damn, Bobby was rubbing off on me. That was a *him* thought if I'd ever heard one.

You call me? Bobby asked in my mind, proving our mental communication network was still in place, though it was kind of one-sided. The power was all his, so unless he was focusing on me, he couldn't hear me if I "spoke." Nice to know he was thinking of me, though, especially after the blond bombshell.

Just thinking of post-mission snogging, I thought back.

You're on. He sent back an image of the two of us locked up in an embrace my parents definitely wouldn't have approved of. Then it cut off abruptly as though something, probably a teacher, had demanded his attention.

I sighed, and the singing girl broke off suddenly, her last note lingering in the air. Her head was as slow to turn as the note was to fade, so I knew my sigh hadn't scared her. Just, it seemed, intruded on her solitude. From her expression, or lack thereof, she turned more because it was expected than because she was actually curious about who or what had come upon her. Her eyes ... if my heart had been beating, it might have stuttered at the sight of them. At first I thought they had to be contacts, they were such a pale ice blue—the color of a frozen lake. Her gaze flicked from Ulric to me, locking on.

"Hello," she said, her speech not nearly as breathy as her song. "I'm Bella."

"Geneva," I answered.

"Cool."

"Bell, where are the others?" Ulric asked as she slithered off the rock, her long black skirt riding up enough to reveal calves nearly as pale as mine.

"Aren't they here?" She looked around with the same lack of concern she'd shown at our approach.

"Did you lose them again?" he asked, as if it were a common joke.

"I guess so," she said with a shrug. Was I seeing some of that lack of energy and focus we'd been briefed on or was Bella just a little ... different?

"Come on," Ulric said, taking Bella's arm gently. "Let's get you to class."

She went quietly, and I trailed after them, already intrigued.

3

By sixth period I was cursing the Feds with every fiber of my being. What good was eternal life if you had to spend it *in school*? And it totally sucked being the new kid because teachers wanted to quiz you on what you already knew and do due diligence getting you up to speed and all that. And then there were the girls who tried to establish dominance over you—because everyone knows the new girl is automatically hot, at least until the novelty wears off, and that totally ticks off some folks.

Speak of the devil—between me and my locker stood Bobby's bleached blond bimbo and her entourage. I thought of Becca and Marcy with a pang. Luckily, it was in character for me to totally ignore the posse's existence and breeze on by, just as it was probably in blondie's nature not to let that happen.

"Hey, new girl," she called as I passed. "Don't you know Halloween's still a month away?"

I had to fight not to bare my teeth. She reminded me of Tina, my archnemesis from my old school, right up to choosing the most obvious put-down in the book, given that I'd gone goth. So, no points for originality. Maybe Bobby would look, but surely he wouldn't touch…

"That all you got?" I asked. "'Cause I have just two words for you—bleach pen."

When she looked totally blank, I brushed my little pinky finger across my brows and watched her go scarlet. Well, all except for those brows, which were at least two shades darker than the hair on her head.

I licked my index finger and air-scored a point for me, making a sizzle sound as I did it.

Blondie flung her hair around as if to fan me away and marched off with her gaggle of gaping groupies, all shooting me dirty looks. Ah, the mean girls. Got it.

During my extensive high school experience, which couldn't be properly replicated in any kind of controlled spy school setting, I'd noticed that mean girls could be identified by the following:

- the height of their noses in the air, which is inversely proportional to the length of their skirts

- their brows, which are so often raised that they disappear into their hairlines (this helps disguise the effects of Botox and facelifts later in life, since no one will ever have seen their brows at resting height)

- they travel in packs, and

- they think *ohmagod* is an actual word, totally to be used as often as humanly possible.

In my old life, I'd been a fashionista. There was a difference. I'd only been trying to beautify, not belittle, the world one person at a time.

Anyway, I ignored them, as I did the guys in the hallway checking out my legs, and made for my locker when someone fell into step with me. I looked up into the leaf-green eyes of a girl dressed much like me, which is to say in black, though her dress was kind of gauzy with red ribbons crisscrossing over the chest, giving it the appearance of a corset, only she was so slim there wasn't much for the bodice to push and smoosh. Her hair was nearly white blond, the natural way, except for where she'd added streaks of what looked like burgundy that had faded to a kind of brassy pink. All of it was stick straight. She looked like emo Barbie, only without the absurd proportions.

"That was pretty wicked," she said. "Gotta admire

anyone who can shut Hailee down. I'm Lily, by the way. Ulric's already told us all about you."

"That couldn't have taken long," I muttered. How much could he know?

"Oh, you'd be surprised," she said, as if reading my mind. "Ulric knows trouble when he sees it, and he says you're all that."

"And more," I added, smiling to let her know it was a joke...kind of.

"Anyway, so you're Geneva," she went on. "And next period you have study hall, right?"

I must have narrowed my eyes.

"Ulric again," she explained. "Photographic memory. So, wanna blow?"

"What?"

She rolled her eyes at me. "What do they call it where you're from? Cut? Skip? Ditch? Bail?"

"Those'll do. But I'm kind of new here. I should probably make it to my classes at least once."

"Why?" she asked.

I thought for a second. "Just seems like the thing to do."

"Right," she said, slipping a hand through my arm like we were either best buds or about to start a hoedown. "Come with me."

I didn't know what it was about grabby goths, but between her and Ulric, they seemed perfectly prepared to lead me around by the nose. If I had a ring through it, they'd probably attach a leash. At least they'd accepted me as one of their own. My cover would have sucked rocks without it.

I knew exactly where we were headed before we even got there. It had to be the hearse front and center of the student parking lot. It stood out from the other cars like a Kate Spade handbag in a sea of knockoffs ... or maybe that should be a knockoff in a sea of Kate Spade bags. I'd totally never understood modern art, and this car was no exception. It was black with eyes painted on the headlights and oversized fangs mounted on the front bumper. Baby-doll heads, each different, were hot-glued to the hood all around its perimeter. Some had red eyes and fangs, others an eye-patch or pirate bandana. Some were painted like werewolves or zombies or even Frankenstein's monster. It was ... surreal.

My steps slowed as we approached, even though I was already starting to feel the sun sizzle on my skin. It was playing peekaboo from behind a cloud, but like the spitball bully from the back of the class, it made itself known.

"Quite a ... car," I said finally, because I was all about diplomacy, especially the kind that came with little ribbons meaning school's out forever.

Lily had been studying my face, waiting for my reaction. "Yeah, and that's just what they've done with the outside. Wait until you see the inside."

"I can hardly wait," I answered, trying for sincerity.

She laughed, and it was high and tinkly. Not at all the sort of Wednesday Addams, psycho-killer laugh I thought goths should sport. "Oh, don't worry, the guys did the chassis mostly to piss off Principal Connolly. She threatened to have it banned from the school lot, so Bram and Byron did a makeover, called it art, and threatened to start a freedom of expression ruckus. Got the ACLU involved and all...Of course, that was before..." She trailed off sadly.

"Before what?"

Instead of answering, she yanked open one of the back doors and the sweet, sharp, unmistakable scent of weed nearly knocked me on the ass-phalt. If I hadn't been pretending to breathe, it probably wouldn't have hit me so hard, but between that and my super-vamp senses, it was the practical equivalent of pepper spray. My nose ran, my eyes watered, and I quickly wiped the moisture away before Lily could tell it was blood, a totally grody side effect of becoming a blood-sucking fiend.

"Climb in," she said.

I could have told her I had my own wheels, but she had me curious, so I did what she said. As the haze started to clear, I noticed two things. First was a guy who looked like he'd stepped out of an Anne Rice novel—poet shirt, pants tight enough that I could practically tell his religion, long hair in a girly-cut. I mean, had anyone *really* rocked that hairstyle since Fabio? Well...maybe Hugh Jackman in *Van Helsing*. Second was that the hearse was set up like a limo inside, with bench seats facing each other for most of its length. The seats were a microfiber that mimicked suede—black, of course. Except for the windows, rug, and seats, words were shellacked everywhere: the ceiling, the spaces between windows, the dashboard...It looked like someone had ripped pages out of books or artistically torn fancy printed passages to use as wallpaper. I'd never seen anything like it.

"*Because I could not stop for death—*" I read.

"He kindly stopped for me," Poet Boy continued. "The carriage held but just ourselves and Immortality."

Okay, I was poetically tone-deaf, but even I could tell that was pretty good. "Wow, did you write that?" I asked. I could see right away it was the wrong thing to say.

Poet Boy barked out a laugh, and I was about to quote my shirt, *Bite Me*, when Lily's tinkling laugh joined his. "He wishes. This one's his." She pointed to one of the torn print-outs. "Tragic death, be still thy heart, and keep thee true once we part. As in death, though not in life, I turn the tables with a twist of the knife."

I thought about that for a second, a little squicked out by the sentiment. You'd have thought *they'd* gone vamp by the way they were holding their breath. "Sounds more like a spell to me. But, uh, nice rhyme scheme."

Lily and Poet Boy exchanged a look, and then he shrugged. "Not much difference really. Spells don't actually need to rhyme, but it helps you remember them."

Okay, that was kind of unexpected. Not a confession, but…I tried not to let my reaction show. "Cool. Maybe you can teach me. I've dabbled, but never really gotten any results."

"Yeah, I'm kind of a dabbler myself," Poet Boy admitted. "Bram's the one you want to talk to. He swears he's seen books bleed."

"With or without pharmaceutical aid?" Lily asked, a

bite to her voice. But she didn't wait for an answer, and I figured it was an old riff. "*Anyway*, Byron, this is Geneva, the one Ulric told us about. Geneva, this is Byron, our resident poet and artist. Bram—"

"Did someone take my name in vain?" asked a new guy, popping his head in through the open door. With four— well, three, and Bram's head—in the back of the hearse, it was starting to get crowded. The newcomer was the rich, warm color of a mochachino, with a shaved head that was absolutely the perfect shape for it. And trust me, not all heads are created equal. He sported deep, dark, kohl-lined eyes and cheekbones that would cut glass. "Beautiful" is not supposed to apply to men, but that was exactly the word for him. If only he weren't wearing enough hardware to open a store.

"Not yet, but give me time," Lily said.

Bram smiled, his canines as long and pointy as I'd ever seen on a non-vamp. I wondered if he filed them or wore falsies. "Thanks for the introduction," he said wryly, holding out a hand to shake. I noticed that his nails were bitten to the quick, and his brick red polish was chipped and cracked. I was glad to see the imperfections.

"The gang's all here," called a voice from behind us— Ulric's, if I wasn't mistaken.

"Which is a good thing," added yet another voice, also masculine, "because I saw VP Feintuch headed this way. We'd better bolt."

Byron tossed Bram a set of keys with a rope-wrapped ball bearing as the fob. "You drive."

"Gavin's got shotgun," Ulric called, pushing Bram aside and wedging himself into the seat beside me. I'd never heard anyone call shotgun for someone else before.

Nobody argued. Everyone scrambled for place like it was a Chinese fire drill, and we were peeling out of the school lot before I even caught an unnecessary breath.

"We're sunk," Gavin complained from the shotgun seat. "It's hard to be inconspicuous in *this*. VP's going to know it was us laying tracks."

In comparison to the others, Gavin looked almost normal—sandy blond-brown hair with overlong bangs, which he kept brushing out of his eyes and tucking behind piercing-free ears; combat boots; jeans; and a T-shirt for the metal band Torrid. Basically, the kind of teen who can be found slouching behind the finest gas station and fast food counters everywhere.

"What's your damage?" Bram asked him.

"I'd actually like to *graduate*," Gavin bit out. "Unlike some of us, I don't have a cushy job in the family business waiting for me when I'm sprung."

"Mortuary," Ulric said, leaning in confidentially with a sly glance at Poet Boy. "Byron's one of *those* Ledbetters."

His breath tickled my ear, and not in a totally ick way.

"New in town, remember. No idea who they are."

"I see dead people," Lily quipped, like that would make it all clear.

"Oh, shut it," Byron snapped. "Anyway, the gang's *not* all here. Where's Bella?"

With the exception of Bram, everyone looked at Lily,

like it was the girls' job to keep track of each other. "What? It wasn't my day to watch her," she answered. "Bram?"

I couldn't see his face, but the Bald and the Beautiful's tone had "sheepish" written all over it. "She ditched me after lunch. I haven't seen her since."

"Um, guys, remember me—the new girl? Completely lost here."

That look went around, the one that passes from person to person in groups where everyone knows each other so well that they can ask and answer questions without speaking. This one, no doubt, had to do with whether to let the outsider in on their secrets. It was Lily who finally answered, with a roll of her eyes. "Boys, she's going to figure it out sooner or later." *Paydirt.* "Bella's got...kind of a love/hate relationship with food." *Or not.* "We try to keep an eye on her, but..."

I blinked. "Huh?" Brilliant interrogation technique, stupidity was.

Lily looked pained; Bram took pity on her and cut in. "Bella's bulimic. She's probably hiding out from us, praying to the porcelain god."

"Very poetic," Lily said, leaning across the rest of us to slap his shoulder.

He shrugged. "What would you prefer? Puke? Vomit? Spew? Blow chunks? Toss cookies? Oh, wait, I have it— reverse peristalsis."

"Ack, enough," I broke in. "Unless you want to see what *I* had for lunch." Virgin Bloody Mary, or Suzy or, hell, Gustav. Courtesy of Uncle Sam. If anyone asked, I'd have told them it was a protein shake. I wouldn't even have been lying. Blood was totally protein, right?

"Not on my carpet!" Byron nearly squeaked.

"I was thinking of your shirt," I told him. "It would make an interesting ink blot, and we could play Name Your Neurosis on the way to wherever we're going."

Lily nearly choked with laughter.

"You interested in psychology?" Ulric asked, his leg brushing mine as he shifted in his seat, then gone again before I could protest.

I shrugged. "As much as anything."

"*Forensic* psychology?" Gavin asked from the front seat.

Could you psychoanalyze dead people? Did the Feds have a division for that? "Um, sure," I said convincingly. "Any kind of abnormal psych." Like there was any other kind. People were weird, even the sane ones.

"Cool. I'm destined to be a CSI guy myself."

"Like blood and fingerprints and all that?" I asked, wondering how to get the conversation back around to spells and the supernatural.

I hadn't paid any attention to where we were going until a sudden stop threw Ulric into my lap and visions of my death played in my head like poisonous sugar plums. I never woke screaming in the night from post-traumatic stress—because I now slept the sleep of the dead—but put me in a car, rattle it around a little...

"Damn, Derek!" Bram hollered, pounding on the steering wheel.

"What the hell was that?" Byron asked.

"That idiot Derek cut us off. He and some other kid are drag racing, and we were in their way."

"Isn't anyone in school?" I asked, voice faint because I could barely suck in a breath.

Ulric shrugged. "New school policy. Attendance is kind of optional."

· · ·

Party central, it turned out, was an outcropping of graffitied rocks overlooking the Hudson River. You had to … get this … *climb* to get there, and lord help you if you teetered too close to the edge. The kicker—no outdoor plumbing. Not so much as a Porta-John in sight. Totally barbaric. Plus, there was the whole sunlight issue. I stepped carefully over broken glass, crushed cans, rolling papers, and stubs of various kinds and found a shady spot to plant myself. My little pleated skirt rode up to pop-diva-exiting-limo length, and Ulric planted himself across from me to take full advantage.

"Subtle," I said dryly. "Sure you don't want to take a picture? It'll last longer."

He smirked, whipped out his cell phone, and snapped a photo before I could protest, and I sat stunned for a full second thinking *damn, damn, damn* before I launched myself at him.

He stood up. Even in my platform Mary Janes I was no match for his height, and I refused to jump for it. I settled for a glare. He was going to be in for a really rude surprise when he tried to check the pic later on. Bobby'd probably have some cool Dark Knight monologue ready about being doomed to walk the shadows or some such thing. All I had was my sense of irony, which, whatever Alanis Morissette says, is *not* a black fly in your chardonnay.

"If that shows up anywhere on the Internet, you're dead meat," I told him. Let him think he'd misaimed the camera when he checked the pic later.

"Nope, this is for my private stash," he answered with a wink.

I told myself that he wasn't at all charming. Obnoxious, overbearing, and obvious, yes. Way too cocky for his own good, check. Vaguely hunkalicious, no.

Two more cars pulled off onto the dirt track created by way too many past vehicles off-roading, and we were joined shortly by three more kids from school who'd apparently brought a "party in a bag"—a six pack of beer; really, really cheap vodka; and more of Byron's very special air freshener.

I didn't want to be a killjoy, but, "Can't the cops spot us up here?" I asked.

Ulric moved to put an arm around me, like I might actually be afraid and in need of masculine reassurance. As if. "They roust us about once a month. We're not due for another couple of weeks. No worries."

More and more people, some bearing pizza and other munchies, showed up as the night went on, and I started to wonder where all *their* parents thought they were. Mine, real or imagined, were out of the picture, but back in Ohio they would have blown a gasket if I'd ditched school and partied the night away. Did these kids have their folks trained? Was the lethargy catching?

Ulric had barely left my side all night, but the others had drifted away little by little. Bram thought he'd seen Bella, and he and Byron—the B Boys—went to search her out. Lily and Gavin crept off on their own a short time later.

"You guys do this every night?" I shouted to Ulric over the boom box someone had brought. It was blasting out something with a base beat so heavy I couldn't hear anything else. And if *I* couldn't hear it…

What I *could* hear was giving me a pounding headache, and I so wished I could numb the pain with the booze I kept pouring out onto the ground. Back during spy school training, a bunch of us had snuck out to party only to come practically face-to-face with our internal organs when our bodies tried to turn themselves inside out. Apparently, when they said variety was the spice of *life*, they meant it literally. Death was a crash diet waiting to happen.

"Nope," Ulric answered in my ear.

"That's it—nope?"

"The word goes out—where, when, etc., and we show up. Simple as that."

"So who sends the word?"

He grabbed my hand and started leading me away from the thick of things. When I balked, he said, "Relax. I'm taking you somewhere we can hear ourselves think. Unless you've got other ideas." He waggled his pierced brow at me, and I smirked before I could catch myself.

"Parcheesi," I answered.

"Strip Parcheesi?"

I sneered.

"A purist. I respect that," Ulric said. "Poker's better for that anyway."

I could kind of hear him now, without him being close enough to kiss. I wondered what Bobby was doing and hoped it didn't involve the blond bombshell, Hailee. If she was the mean-girl equivalent of the old me, she wouldn't be caught dead at a party sans indoor plumbing and mirrors for makeup reapplication. Mochas at the mall would be more her scene, and Bobby probably wouldn't be within a hundred miles of the mall. Unless they were having an electronics sale.

I leaned against a tree to keep Ulric and me from separating any further from the pack and did my best to focus on my questioning. For some reason, that focus was a little tricksy ... er, tricky. "So, word went out? Party among the pines?"

"More or less. We can't fall into a pattern or the cops'll know when to bust us, but on a Wednesday night at Red Rock—who's looking?"

"But you guys come here often?"

"What're you, a narc?" he asked, not looking truly suspicious yet, but clearly keeping the option open.

"Nope." I shook my head, and it seemed extra wobbly, like I'd become a bobble-head doll. The world took an extra beat or two to settle back into place. "I'm a girl. Pretty sure you've noticed."

Ulric's eyes lit up at that, and he went from leaning against his own tree to taking a step closer to mine.

"Uh oh," I giggled.

He stopped, giving me a hard look. "You okay?"

Another giggle escaped before I clapped my hands to my mouth. Did goths giggle? Oh, crap.

"You're high!" Ulric said, amusement chasing the intensity from his face.

I thought for a second. Fought for thought, like I was a poet and didn't even know it. The world wouldn't hold still. Maybe all this breathing was making my head spin. Vamps weren't equipped for it. And the Mary Jane in the air...Mary Jane, just like my shoes! I giggled again. Contact high...as the sky.

"Yup!" I answered happily. "You?"

He shook his head.

"Don't *you* breathe?" It was out of my mouth before my brain kicked in, and I covered my mouth with both hands like the words hadn't already escaped.

Ulric looked at me funny again. "You're not a straight-edger, are you? Crap, I never figured you for one."

"A what?" I asked, baffled.

And suddenly a scream pierced the night.

4

I bucked myself off the tree and immediately caught my heel on a root, nearly going face first into the dirt. Damn shoes. I kicked them off, thinking the forest could totally reclaim them for all I cared, and sprinted toward the sound, leaving Ulric behind to "What the hell?" me.

He caught up quickly and grabbed my shoulder, but I yanked it away again, still running but remembering not to go full bore. *Faster than a speeding bullet, more powerful than a locomotive…* probably a dead giveaway that I was different. *Get it, DEAD giveaway?* I asked myself. I told the toasted comic in my brain to shut it.

"Are you crazy?" Ulric asked, gulping for breath as he fought not to fall behind. "Do you know how much broken glass there is around here? Not to mention snakes."

I stumbled at the thought of tiny fangs piercing my foot. Even a poisonous snake wouldn't kill me, but it might slow me down and blow me up like a balloon before my natural vamp healing could kick in. I could battle baddies in that state if I had to, but it wouldn't be an elegant ass-kicking. And I was all about style.

I didn't realize how fast I was going until I nearly collided with someone as we hit the core gathering, and barely had time to adjust. I stayed upright by ping-ponging off other people like a pinball...

Only to be stopped by a jock wall.

I smelled the blood even before I saw it. By using Ulric's shoulder to support myself and standing on my tiptoes, I could see a battered Bella just beyond the jocks. Her eyes were no longer fey, but wild and furious. The blood came from a cut on her swelling cheek.

"What's going on?" I asked a kid nearby who was just watching, his cell phone held at the ready as if to get a picture rather than dial 911.

He didn't look away to answer. "I guess Nat gave the emo girl a ride up here and didn't find her properly appreciative."

"So he hit her?" I asked, outraged.

He shrugged. "She spilled beer on his kicks when she pushed him away."

I couldn't decide who to take down first—the jocks or this jerk, who seemed to find spilled beer a good reason for bloodshed—but I was going to have to figure it out fast. My eyeteeth were growing at the blood-scent and the ugly energy that filled the air. Jerky boy wasn't the only one watching expectantly.

"You bastard!" Bram cried, barreling out of nowhere on the far side of the crowd to grab Bella and put her behind him. Byron was right beside him. "You only beat girls, or you want to try me on for size?"

"With all those earrings, who can tell the difference?" Jock-itch answered.

Bram launched himself at the bully boy, who side-stepped and grabbed Bram's arm as he flew past. I heard a pop like his shoulder coming out of the socket, and then Bram was being whirled like a wrecking ball straight at Byron. Jock-itch released him at just the right moment and Bram struck Byron with a terrible thud, both collapsing to the ground. That was *it*. I pushed through the jock wall using all my super strength and leapt into the action. I jump-kicked Jock-itch's arm at the elbow, cringing at the snap as something gave way. He never even saw me coming.

One of his partners in crime grabbed a pigtail and nearly yanked it out of my head before I hit him with a sharp elbow to the groin. He cried out and buckled, but caught my bare foot as he hit the ground and twisted my leg out from under me. I went crashing down to my knees.

As soon as my flesh hit the ground, lightning seemed to arc through me, as though I'd landed on an exposed power line grounding itself through my body. Pure, crackling energy sizzled through me and every synapse, every muscle, hell, even my bones seemed to be electrocuted and as tense and taut as a tripwire.

Ulric tried to put himself between me and the jocks, to protect me while I was down, but they saw their chance at me. Bram and Byron hadn't reentered the fight; I had only a second to worry about why not before a jock was pole-vaulting Ulric to get at me and his friend was lunging from the other direction.

I roared upward, catching one of the guys with an uppercut to the jaw and another with my shoulder to his stomach. He buckled over me and I used his momentum, thrusting him toward his still-reeling friend. They landed hard and went rolling, one over the other … right toward the sudden drop-off of Red Rock. Rather than stop them, everyone pulled back, afraid to be caught up and carried over the cliff themselves. Panic gripped me, and between the adrenaline and the weird electricity flooding my system, I flew into overdrive. I dove for them, tackling their legs and shredding my shirt before I was able to halt their slide and stop them cold. All the fight had gone out of them.

For a second, the whole world froze. Then I heard a "Whoa!" from the crowd, and the sound of sobbing and Bram's name being called more and more frantically.

Shaky from adrenaline overload, I got to my feet and

made myself limp over to my gang, even though my scuffed-up knees were already healing beneath my trashed stockings. My legs nearly went out from under me as I took in the devastation. Byron, scraped but whole, held a trembling, sobbing Bella to his chest. Ulric, on the ground and fighting to stop his bleeding nose, watched me like he'd just seen me walk on water. And Bram…Bram hadn't moved. Lily, who'd been calling out his name, pushed through the crowd and fell to her knees beside him, heedless of the blood pooling beneath Bram's perfect head where it had landed on a jagged rock. Gavin shoved through the crowd a split second behind her, yelling "Don't!" as it looked like she might hug Bram to her. "Call the paramedics, but don't move him!"

"But we have to stop the bleeding!" she answered.

"You," I said, pointing at the jerk I'd talked to first, who'd lowered his phone now that he'd gotten whatever sick shots he'd wanted, "call an ambulance. Lily, listen to Gavin. You might paralyze him or something if you move him now."

To my horror, I spoke with a lisp. I'd forgotten the fangs. With all the blood, they weren't retracting any time soon. But only Ulric was watching me. The others…they were focused on Bram or Bella. I fought for control over myself.

"If I hadn't twisted as we fell, he'd have landed on me," Byron said into the stunned silence. "I'd have broken his fall."

Kids were already melting away, not wanting to deal with the paramedics or the cops who might come with.

"Or maybe it would have been your head on the rock,"

I said, no patience for the blame game. The adrenaline or whatever had kicked me into a frenzy was starting to wear off, leaving me snappish ... and hungry. The thirst warred with horror over the cause ... my friends' blood. I should go, before Ulric's gushing nose started to look like a champagne fountain. Ewww, definitely well before that. But I couldn't leave, not with Bram so helpless and with no idea whether the violence was magically inspired or whether it would start up again the second my back was turned. *Something* was going on. The electrified feeling that had zipped through me when my knees hit the ground was proof of that.

·   ·   ·

It seemed like forever and a day before the ambulance came, and by then all but the fallen had bugged out. One of the paramedics made a call while his partner got right to work. I suspected that given the damage, the under-aged victims, and the party paraphernalia, they wanted some back-up. Probably police. I nearly cried as I watched Bram being loaded onto a backboard to keep him stiff and avoid spinal injuries like Gavin had been worried about, and then tucked away into the ambulance. But I kept the tears in better than my teeth. I'd learned months ago that I wept blood, and that wasn't a sight anyone needed to see. Guilt sucked at me like a Hoover. I should have been able to protect Bram and Bella. I should have been keeping an eye on them all rather than wandering off with Ulric. The fact that they'd wandered off first didn't make me feel any better.

"Where're your shoes?" Lily asked, having, like me, slid off to the fringes to get out of the way of the medics.

I shrugged. "Dunno."

"Hear you kicked serious ass."

"Is there any other kind?" I asked, working hard to hide my pointy teeth. "You didn't see?"

It was her turn to shrug.

"I don't know," I answered. "I was so extra crispy I just kind of went nuts when I saw the jocks picking on Bella."

Sirens sounded in the distance. "We'd better blow," she said, grabbing my arm in an iron death-grip.

Byron was watching us, and some kind of sign passed between them. He got the others moving.

The paramedics looked like they would have stopped us, but had their hands full. We bolted for the totally conspicuous hearse.

If I was lucky, being so new to the group and all, no one would immediately think to give up my name when the cops traced the car ... unless that whole butt-whupping thing stuck in people's heads as, you know, it kinda might.

Everyone was subdued on the drive back to the school lot to drop me off at my car. And it wasn't a peaceful silence. By the pulse-point on her neck, I could see that Lily's heart was beating against her chest like a caged bird. It was distracting. With all the energy I'd burned, I was almost desperate to feed, and while I'd prefer a nice juicy slab of beefcake, angel food was starting to look pretty good right about then.

A trickle of blood down Lily's snowy skin would look like strawberry sauce, and her white-blond hair almost put me in mind of whipped topping.

I licked my lips, and when Ulric stared, I explained, "Chapped."

Of course, I was probably in the one car in the whole school where if I'd asked, someone might actually have opened a vein for me. Byron might even write a poem about it.

I ignored the temptation, pretending I wasn't shaky with need. Once back to my own car, I could make it home in less then ten minutes. The Feds had provided a refrigerator's worth of bottled blood. Five seconds after the infusion, I planned to be on the phone to agents Stick and Stuffed. Whatever had happened back at Red Rock hadn't been natural—not the attack, the spectators, or even me.

5

I woke up the next morning still reeking of smoke and blood. Last night, after downing a bottle and a half of totally grody congealed blood that I'd been way too tired to heat to acceptability, I'd done a face plant on the lumpy mattress and gone out before I could make the intended call.

I nearly fell out of bed when I awoke, flailing like I'd been falling to my death in my dreams, which was really weird, since I hadn't had any dreams since I'd turned. I guessed that for humans, dreams were the subconscious working overtime, but for us vamps, sleep was more about *losing* consciousness, practically dying for hours at a time and coming back to life again. Normally, our lights went out when the sun came up, but the potion the Feds had introduced into our bottled blood was messing with the natural order of things, and my body was rebounding.

Anyway, I tried to get a mental message to Bobby about the events of last night—so much harder to trace and eavesdrop on mind-speak than on cell calls—but no one was answering. That wasn't unusual, since Bobby had to be actively listening for me in order for our brainwave radio to work. Still, I was a little miffed that maybe I wasn't the first thing on his mind in the morning.

I decided I'd try to call the old fashioned way once I'd had a shower and burned the clothes I was in, because I couldn't stand myself a second longer. I'd never actually washed my own clothes—Mom had always had our laundry picked up, done, and delivered. It seemed easier to buy new than try to figure it out for myself. Maybe I'd even go green and recycle my duds or something by dumping them into a donation bin. There had to be people out there with more need than fashion sense.

I shed clothes as I walked to the shower, but the apartment was so small I still had my skivvies on when I hit the bathroom. I figured the easiest way to salvage my matching bra and panties, the only decent parts of my ensemble, would be to wash them with me, so I started the water running and walked in, bra, undies, and all.

I felt much better once I emerged, leaving the black bikini to drip dry. Mischievously, I tried Bobby again as I stood there in my towel and nothing else. This time he answered.

Gina?

Ask me what I'm wearing, I said.

Um, hold on. It wasn't exactly the reaction I was going for.

Sorry, had to close the door. So, what are you wearing?

Nothing. I left out the towel, because, really, that was need to know, and he didn't. *Want to sneak out of the mom-and-pop shop?*

More than you know, but that would make us late for school.

I rolled my eyes. That's what I got for dating a geek. I gave him a mental raspberry, which, being spit-free, was not terribly effective. *Spoilsport. Anyway, I'm really just here to check in.* Mostly.

I poured it all out—the party, the attack, the witnesses to my kick-assitude. Thankfully, I could probably convince people that what they'd seen was some kind of drug-induced hallucination, if push came to shove. I mean, little ole me whupping up on the big, bad jocks? As if.

Bobby treated my monologue to a thoughtful silence. Then, *You be careful. I don't like you being in the middle of all this.*

It warmed my unbeating heart, but at the same time seemed a bit chauvinistic. *I went through the same training you did.*

I know, but I can't help feeling like I got you into all this and I just … worry.

Aww, that was so sweet. His bite *had* kind of set me on the path to unlife, but I hadn't exactly been protesting at the time.

If you're feeling that badly, I know how you can make it up to me, I teased. *Diamonds* are *a girl's best friend, after all.*

I could practically hear him gulp right through our mental link. *Diamonds … really?*

I was going soft at my young age. *Okay, maybe I'm more of a rubies and sapphires kind of girl. I'm all about color. But don't tell anyone. I have a high-maintenance rep to maintain.*

Your secret's safe with me. He promised to talk to "Mom" and "Dad" (aka Stick and Stuffed) about the goings on and get back to me about whatever they discovered.

He signed off and I sighed, contemplating another day as Dawn of the Dead. I turned the TV to news while I got ready. It wasn't my usual, but I only got four semi-clear channels anyway and I wanted to see if the news had anything about Bram's condition on it. They were on a story about some totally contested political campaign, as if *that* was news. I was in the closet when I heard, " … leaving several kids hurt, two missing, and one in a coma."

I froze. *Coma!*

"The police investigation is ongoing. Chief Reilly had this to say—"

I stepped out of the closet in time to see a burly man

with jowls and a buzz cut standing in front of a podium, flashbulbs going off around him.

"We're doing everything we can to locate the missing teens. Search parties started at sunup this a.m. At this time, we're asking anyone with information to call the number below." An 800 number scrolled across on a ticker along the bottom of the screen. "In addition, we've made it a priority to crack down on these underage parties. Known locations will have an increased police presence."

A female reporter at the front of the pack shouted down her peers. "Would you comment on the curfew that's been discussed?"

Chief Reilly looked momentarily nonplussed. "I don't think we've yet reached the point of making this a police state, do you? Next question."

I didn't hear any more. My mind was already reeling. *Coma.* I wasn't a med head, but based on what I'd seen, that had to be Bram. Brave, multi-pierced Bram, who'd only been trying, far as I could tell, to protect Bella. My heart, with nothing better to do, not having to beat and all, ached. But only for Bram. I probably should worry about the guys I'd hurt in his defense. They might have been under some kind of influence, but ... nope, I just couldn't care.

But who on earth was missing? Everyone had faded away like smoke at the 911 call. How could the police have determined anything in last night's insanity? Maybe the kids' parents had reported them missing. Or ... a horrible, horrible thought occurred to me. Could the whole smackdown have been a distraction for a kidnapping? I didn't know what that might or might not have to do with our mission, but... Well, dammit, if someone had suckered me into a rumble to cover for them, they were going to pay.

•   •   •

School was weird. For one thing, the hearse was nowhere in sight when I pulled into the lot... late, because I kept waiting for the news to come back around to the incident at Red Rock. Unfortunately, the top of the hour had rolled around to crappy chat-news format, where special guests demonstrated new exercise techniques or talked about websites where parents could get rankings on kids' games based on drugs, sex, and language, as if we didn't hear all that at school. It was amazing what they called news these days. Glorified infomercials.

My sneer lasted until I hit the lobby and saw Lily and Bella in a huddle. Bella certainly looked a lot less bloody and more alert than I'd last seen her, but her cheek was still swollen, and now a vivid purple as well.

"Oh, Gen," Lily started as soon as she saw me. "It's so awful—they took Byron and Gavin right out of home-room."

"They?"

"The cops," Bella said, in that whispery voice of hers.

Right, not everything is about vampires and juju.

"Just for questioning," Lily was quick to add. "But still, Byron and Gavin aren't exactly their favorite all-American boys."

"So they haven't come for you two or Ulric?" I asked, showing my firm grasp of the obvious.

"Not yet," she answered.

"It's all my fault. They were fighting over *me*," Bella moaned suddenly, her eyes huge in her pinched face. Her eyes were, in fact, the only things about her that could be called huge, unless it was her sense of drama. I seriously wanted to get the girl a Valium or a sandwich, whichever would do the most good. She looked like one of those ridiculous Manga girls you could snap in half as easily as a Twix bar. If she was praying to the porcelain god, as the gang seemed to think, she couldn't be offering much in the way of tribute.

"Bella, they were fighting *for* you," Lily said, reading my mind. "There's a difference. Anyway, it's about time someone showed those guys they can't just take whatever they want. They never even saw Gen coming!"

I blushed, and wondered what that looked like on my bone-white face. *That's right*, I thought, *Geneva Belfry, Supergoth.* I could picture the black bat-winged cape, the killer knee-high boots with three-inch titanium heels. The better to beat you with. Wouldn't Bobby just love it?

"It was the adrenaline," I lied. "I probably couldn't do it again in a million years."

For a second, Lily looked ancient and knowing, but she only said, "Whatever happened, I'm sure they'll get to questioning us sooner or later. About last night, the missing kids—"

"Missing?" Bella asked, her voice rising a whole octave. "Who's missing? I haven't heard a thing."

"They said something on the news," Lily volunteered, "but they haven't released the names."

The second bell rang and Bella nearly jumped out of her skin, which, now that I think about it, is a totally morbid expression.

"Gotta go," she squeaked, hurrying off like a mouse.

Lily and I exchanged a look. "Don't ask me," she said. "Bella's a mystery wrapped in an enigma."

"Huh?"

"You know, weird."

Oh yeah, weird was something with which I had a close personal relationship.

•   •   •

Part of me wanted to head for the hospital, despite the fact that hospitals gave me hives—a polyester allergy, maybe, or an aversion to those cutesy scrubs with suns and moons and the dish running away with the spoon. It was kind of hard to trust the credentials of a nurse wearing the latest in *Goodnight Moon*.

Anyway, it just seemed wrong to focus on stupid things like *learning* when so much *real* stuff going on—police interrogations, missing kids, Bram's coma. And even wronger to be asked to focus without caffeine. I'd about kill for an espresso. Maybe I could insist that my next shipment of blood be tapped from the veins of a caffeine addict. Or maybe I could find a roommate to provide my blood hot and fresh every morning, like a Dunkin' Donuts counter in my very own home. I wondered how I'd word *that* ad:

Roommate wanted. Free rent in exchange for
bloodletting. Apply with photo and sample.

Hmm…

It took a minute to realize that my whole homeroom was staring at me, and an extra second for reality to penetrate and my little fantasy to fade away. Mr. Richardson's pug eyes made his glower particularly effective.

"You're smiling," he accused me.

I gave him a blank look.

"I was talking about the events of last night, saying we'd have a counselor on hand to deal with the shock and grief. You were grinning like an idiot."

There was something ugly in his tone, but I guess I could understand that.

"What were you thinking about, Ms. Belfry?" he asked, eyes trying to burn a hole through my head. But I'd done hand-to-hand combat with creepy psycho-psychics before the Feds ever found me and was not going to be intimidated by a Podunk professor. "Perhaps you can share with the class."

"Coffee," I answered. "But if I had enough to share with the class, I wouldn't be daydreaming about it."

The class laughed, breaking the tension a bit but pissing off Richardson, who turned away, muttering something about brain-dead kids and how he might as well mark us *all* absent, just like our minds.

I almost made it to third period before Ulric ambushed me in the hall outside art class, which Agents Stick and Stuffed had arranged for me, apparently not realizing that I hadn't progressed beyond stick figures. (In their defense, I was *fabu* with a color wheel.) Lily and Bella were with him. "We're ditching to visit Bram at the hospital. You with us?"

I looked at each of them. Bella was staring at her toes. Lily was looking back at me, some kind of plea in her eyes, but I had no idea for what. I debated what to do. On the one hand, I was worried about Bram and up for any excuse to ditch class. On the other ... at the rate I was going—or *not* going—to my classes, I might be kicked out of school before I had the chance to figure out what the heck was going on with these people. I didn't think the Feds would look kindly on me flunking my first mission, and I wasn't anxious to find out how they might go about terminating my services. Plus, there was the whole hospital-hives deal. I should probably stay behind.

Yeah, probably, but when had I ever done the smart thing? Besides, this might be my only chance to question the jerky jocks while they were stuck in hospital beds hopped up on pain meds. I just hoped they weren't still upset about their butt-whupping. It'd just break my heart if they popped their stitches trying to get at me. Of course, a broken heart wasn't exactly fatal in my line of work.

What would Kim Possible do? I asked myself. Sadly, I

knew the answer to that. Orderlies and antiseptic wouldn't scare her. She'd follow the leads.

"I should probably make it to my afternoon classes at some point," I waffled, one last time.

Lily let out a breath. "Good, you can stay here with—"

"But I think we should all stick together," I finished.

"—me," Lily trailed off. "What? Why?"

"In case there's another attack," I answered her. "Safety in numbers and all that."

Ulric gave Lily a shark's smile. "You're outnumbered, Lil. Come on, time to face your fears."

"Hospitals give me the heebie-jeebies," she said as an aside to me.

"Oh, sing it, sister," I answered. "But this is for Bram. Maybe hearing our voices will help somehow."

"Bella's anyway," Ulric said. "Her voice could probably make the dead sit up and take notice."

"Don't say 'dead,'" Bella ordered.

"What? I meant that in a good way."

"Uh, guys, if we're going to go, now would be the time." Lily was looking past us down the hall. Instinctively, we all turned to see a woman in a pinstriped pants suit—the principal?—coming at us with two men who practically screamed *detective*.

"Well, they've got our names and faces. We might as well get it over with—" I started.

Bella bolted for the emergency door at the far end of the hall.

"Damn!" Lily and I cried.

We all took off running after her.

"Bella!" Ulric called, but she'd hit the push bar on the exit door and burst out into the sunlight before we could reach her.

We hit it seconds later, almost running into Bella, who now stood on the walkway looking lost.

"My car, this way," I said, pretending to be winded like them.

We raced for the parking lot. My clunker was so old I had to use a key to let myself in and manually open the other locks. It cost us. The principal had stopped at the edge of the lot, but the cops were breathing down our necks one row away when I slammed the car into gear and backed out at ludicrous speed. Bella didn't even have her door fully shut. It scraped against the much nicer car next to mine. I'd pay for it later—Agents Stick and Stuffed would, anyway. I wondered how they'd feel about me running from the law.

"Whoo hoo!" Ulric said as we shot out of the lot like a bat outta hell. "Way to go, Gen."

I rolled my eyes at the rearview mirror. "Yeah, because running from the cops doesn't make us look at all guilty. Bella, what were you thinking?"

"That it's all my fault. I tried to get through the day, but I have to see Bram. To tell him I'm sorry."

"Bella, we keep telling you it *isn't* your fault. You want to blame someone, blame octo-jock," I said.

"Octo-jock?" Ulric asked, amused.

"Yeah, too many tentacles."

"I knew I liked you."

I looked away from the warmth of his smile. I felt good and bad all at the same time. Part of me had the warm fuzzies about being part of a group again. I hadn't realized how much I liked high school and my clique until they were taken away from me, but then I froze up at the remembrance that this was a role I was playing. I couldn't afford friendships that could cloud my judgment, and I'd be moving on when all was said and done. The thought stung more than it should have. These weren't my people, I told myself—no color palette, death poetry, so many piercings I wondered why they didn't spring a leak. It didn't help, but I might as well get used to it. I had an eternal lifetime of good-byes to look forward to.

"I don't know what got into those guys," Lily said. "I mean, Nat's always been a putz, but Kevin's usually pretty decent ... for a jock."

"Something in the water," Ulric answered, joking, but I made a mental note. "A lot of weirdness going on. And I'm not just talking about Lily's love life."

"Bite me, *Toby*," she snapped back. There was silence, and I felt like some kind of line had been crossed. Finally, Lily said, "Sorry."

Ulric nodded tersely, and we sat in silence for the rest of the ride.

6

It was a straight shot up Route 9 and probably wouldn't have taken long if it hadn't been for the zillion traffic lights. We might not have hit them all, but we gave it our best shot. We passed two malls without even turning in, and that almost killed me all over again. I only managed because I was thinking of Bram, his perfect skull bashed in, lying in a coma. I wondered what a sip of vampire blood could do for him. But if we didn't finish the ritual blood exchange, would it kill him? Or make him stronger?

They hadn't covered that in spy school. I doubted it was because they didn't have the answer—they probably knew more about us than we did ourselves.

That was what held us, beyond the fact that the Feds knew our identities and could hunt us down if we chose to bolt instead of cooperate. They knew things they hadn't yet shared. Things like the key to the sunscreen potion used in our bottled blood. Maybe even what Bobby's dam, the wench Mellisande, had done to her own sire Alistaire to twist him nearly beyond recognition, and how to reverse it.

As Alistaire stood when I'd last seen him, as he stood *now*, he was a danger to everyone. A triple threat—psychic, unstoppable, and mad as a hatter—but I couldn't forget that he'd let me live, temporarily anyway. He did sort of imply that all bets were off should our paths cross again. Maybe even that he was going to do his very best to make that happen.

"You think he'll be okay, right?" Bella asked, and for a minute I couldn't think who she was talking about, my thoughts had wandered so far. "And Gavin and Byron too?"

"Bram's going to be fine," I answered, with more certainty than I felt. I couldn't imagine what the police could hold Byron and Gavin on, since neither had thrown a single punch.

"You don't know that," Bella said faintly.

"I have a strong premonition," I said. I had to steer things back around to the arcane somehow. My investigation so far had only led me to more questions. No answers that I could use to barter with the Feds.

"You mean, like a vision?" Lily asked. "I get those sometimes."

"Not as strong as all that, though I wish. Maybe you can work with me, teach me how to get more in touch with my powers."

Lily's eyes shown when I looked into them via the rearview mirror. "Absolutely. Maybe we can try a healing spell for Bram while we're at it."

Bingo, I thought. I wondered if the zippy feeling I'd felt at Red Rock had anything to do with a spell. Hopefully, I'd know soon enough.

• • •

The lady at the hospital reception desk gave us the same look the woman in the school office had given me yesterday. I was tempted to stick out my tongue or cross my eyes, but I behaved myself. For once. After all, we needed her to give up Bram's room number so we didn't wander around aimlessly.

Ulric made the approach, hoping, I think, to charm her. He wore his most wolfish smile as he asked after Bram.

"I'll need names and IDs," the woman said, unimpressed by his charm. Of course, she was old enough to have been on duty the day of his birth, so that might have factored into it.

She directed us to a bank of elevators up to the fifth floor and handed us green visitor passes. They matched my eyes—the passes, not the elevators, which were an industrial gray color, stark against the white walls which were broken two-thirds of the way down by a wide strip of mus-tard yellow that was probably meant to be cheerful. Or to make the visitors look as jaundiced as the patients, so the latter didn't feel so bad.

We were halfway to the elevators when I heard her pick up the phone and say into it, "Four for Thomkins on their way up."

I didn't think any of the others heard, since they didn't have my vamped-out senses. I looked over my shoulder and found the reception lady staring back. "That's right," she said to the person on the other end of the line.

She replaced the receiver, and I knew we were screwed. I figured I could have another of my "premonitions," about what awaited us at the other end of the elevator ride, but running again would only compound the police interest in us. Maybe I could learn something from the questioning, like the identity of the missing kids.

Sure enough, there was an armed officer waiting for us as the elevator doors opened on the fifth floor, though he wisely held off making himself known until the doors slid closed behind us. He *insisted* on escorting us to the visitors' lounge and stood guard outside, promising that someone would be with us shortly. Oh joy, oh rapture.

"Damn it, damn it, damn it," Ulric said, slapping the particleboard table in the midst of the 1970s Day-Glo orange chairs. "Trapped. Although," he said slowly, "three girls, no waiting. I could do worse."

"Dream on, loverboy," Lily answered, with a slap to his arm.

"Go easy on him," I said. "Every lounge needs a lizard."

Ulric clutched his heart and fell, mock-wounded, into the closest chair. Only Bella wasn't joining in. She slumped onto the couch, looking like guilt's poster girl.

We cooled our heels for ten or twenty minutes that felt like a century before the door opened again, letting in the two officers we'd evaded at school. Oh yes, we were criminal masterminds.

I hadn't gotten a good look at the detectives back at school, but now that I had ... well, we had Hunky Cop and his partner Crinkly. Hunky Cop had a scar on his chin, very *Indiana Jones*. Without it, his fine features and long lashes might have hurled him past handsome and into pretty-boy territory. And no one wanted that.

Really. I swear.

His partner had the kind of brush-cut blond hair where you almost can't see the gray. Almost. But you could tell his age from the crinkles—between the brows, up around the eyes, and bracketing the mouth. His face was like a map that had been refolded one too many times. I had supreme sympathy for the collagenically challenged. The old me would have said, "You poor thing, didn't your mama ever teach you to moisturize," but I bit down the urge. Hard. Blood flooded my mouth, and it was so, so wrong that it whetted my appetite for more. Seriously, macking on *myself*? I was officially a mutant.

"Well, kids, I guess you know you're in a lot of trouble," Crinkly Cop began.

"See," said Ulric, slapping me like Lily'd slapped him. "I *told* you we shouldn't have skipped fourth period."

I rolled my eyes. They were getting quite the work-out.

Crinkly ignored him, like he hadn't spoken. "I guess you know we've already talked to your friends. They had quite a lot to say."

"I doubt it," Lily mumbled.

Hunky turned to her. "What was that?"

"Look, they didn't see the fight, okay?" she said vehemently.

"They were there," Crinkly insisted. "We have witnesses."

"No," I said, drawing his attention. "It was all me. The jocks were beating on Bella, and I stepped in to help her. If the jerky jocks say otherwise, they're lying."

Both cops gave me the body check—up and down. I could see them mentally calculating my height and weight, trying to figure out how in the world I could have caused the damage they'd seen. Clearly, they didn't want to discount a confession, but—

"We'd ask them, except one can't say anything at all with his jaw wired shut. The other can't remember."

"Or so he says," Hunky murmured to his partner. "Could be selective amnesia."

"Why? Because I'm a *girl*?" I taunted. It gave away that I could hear him, but he hadn't truly been whispering. Not effectively, anyway.

Hunky looked at me. Again, measuring. "No, because

he's got about fifty pounds on you *and* you're a girl," he answered.

"Sixty at least, but who's counting?" I said. It just slipped out.

To his left, I could see Ulric smile... and then something else caught my attention. In the lounge window, which was blurry with fingerprints smudging the cheap glass, was a face, contorted in anger. *Rick's.* But why? He stared at me, his glare almost hot enough to melt through the glass and scald me.

The officers, their backs to the door, blocking us in, couldn't see him, though Hunky Cop turned to look at my sudden preoccupation.

Rick had disappeared.

"I have to pee," I announced suddenly, thinking that maybe Rick was trying to give me some kind of message. Maybe I could find and talk to him.

Hunky Cop looked back at me suspiciously. "Right now?"

"I can probably wait until I get to the bathroom."

Somehow, he didn't appreciate my humor. "Fine. I'll walk you there."

"And they say chivalry is dead."

He gestured me ahead of him. I looked right and left as we walked, hoping to catch sight of Rick waving me into one of the rooms, though I had no idea how I'd ditch my escort. I didn't see him by the time we hit the rest room, and I didn't see any choice but to go in. No sooner was I through the door than I was slammed up against it, an inch or so of solid wood between me and Hunky Cop outside, who suddenly didn't seem like the enemy.

Hunky pounded on the door. "You okay in there?" he called.

"I just slipped," I called back. "Sorry! Someone spilt water."

I looked into Rick's eyes, which were far too close and crazed. I wanted to thrust him back and demand to know what he thought he was doing, but he had back-up in the form of a redheaded jock in gray sweats and a wife-beater T-shirt. Resigned, I let Rick keep the flaming skull on my T-shirt twisted up in his fist.

"What the hell, dirtwad? This is the *ladies' room*," I said. Luckily, pissed fit both my cover and my mood.

"You put my guys in the hospital," Rick growled. "Nat is eating through a *straw*."

"Dude, *my* guy isn't eating at all, so you can back the hell up."

I'd never seen Rick like this. If he was acting, he was doing a helluva job at it, but I thought this was something more. There was something off, like the crazy violence last night at Red Rock. It had even gotten to me. *I'd broken somebody's jaw.* Only I hadn't felt angry, just...energized. I didn't even know if the jerky jock had really deserved it or if it was some kind of drug or spell that was speaking through his fists.

Rick pulled me toward him and slammed me back against the door again. I heard a manly yelp from outside and knew that Hunky Cop had tried to push his way in during the millisecond my body wasn't blocking the door.

"Police!" he yelled. "I'm coming in."

"The police, man!" the redheaded sweat-child said, as if Rick couldn't hear for himself.

"No worries," Rick answered.

He grabbed me to him again with one hand and flung the door open with the other, pushing me into the shocked cop with enough force that I'd have fallen if he hadn't caught me. Rick and Red made a break for it while the cop's arms were full and his balance was off, bolting down the hall and dodging a gurney in their way. They were gone in a flash.

Hunky Cop twitched like he was priming to run after them, but I grabbed his arms and hugged him, as if I were a shaken little girl in need of reassurance. I didn't know what Rick had been about, but there was no need to expose us both to the cops ... for now.

Hunky held me for another second, until I pretended to stop shivering, then gripped my forearms gently and eased me far enough away to see my face.

"Who were those guys?"

"A couple of jocks," I said. "Ticked off that I'd hurt their friends. I *told* you it was me."

He looked stunned. "Do you know their names?"

I shook my head. "I'm new here. Outside of the goths, I don't really know anyone."

"So you fought for a girl you've just met?" he asked suspiciously.

"Wouldn't you?"

He didn't have an answer for that. He brought me back to his partner, and they questioned us for another twenty minutes or so, but in the end, with only my account of things and no one to cry foul or press charges, there wasn't much they could do. Oh, there'd been beer bottles and whatnot all over the site, but it was too late to check our blood alcohol levels, and unless they fingerprinted us, which in any case would only prove we'd handled the bottles, not that we'd drunk out of them, they were out of luck. But they'd be watching. That was clear enough.

By the time the questioning wound down, I was eying Hunky Cop's neck like a junkie with the midnight munchies. It was his own fault, really. The coffee he'd had right in front of me probably qualified as cruel and unusual punishment. If he'd been drinking mochachinos, he would have gone down. My willpower only stretched so far.

And, of course, I had to decline even the sodas they offered us because of my blood-only diet. But I probably looked totally tough to the others, like "I don't want nothin' from you, Copper."

Finally, Bella moaned, "*Now* can we see Bram?"

The cops took pity on us. "You go with them," Crinkly said to his partner. "I want to talk to the girl a second."

He meant me. I'd faced down worse, though, than a cop in a no-Macy's town. I wasn't worried.

Bella, Lily, and Ulric all looked at me to be sure I was okay with that, and I nodded them on.

"Go," I added. "I'll be right there."

Hunky Copy ushered them out, Ulric shooting me backward glances until the door closed behind them.

"Girl," Crinkly said, calling my attention back to him. "*Geneva.* You're new here, so possibly you don't understand the way things work. If someone's knocking your friend around, you get her out of there. You don't break some guy's jaw and another's arm." He looked stern, implacable, *serious.*

"Yes, sir," I answered, even though it hurt to say it. I'd do it again in a second if I had to, and I knew it.

"Good. Anything else happens and your name comes up, I'm locking you away until I can find something to stick you with—jaywalking, underage drinking, fake ID. I don't like it when trouble rolls into my town."

He sounded like he was straight out of the old west, but I was smart enough not to crack a smile.

"Understood."

And finally, *finally* he led me to the others. To Bram.

Ulric tapped Lily on the shoulder, and they both shifted away from Bram's bedside far enough to make room for me. I thought Ulric needed a second, anyway. He pretended to cough into his sleeve, but I saw him use it to wipe away a tear. I was touched that they'd give up a place for me at the bedside when I really didn't belong. I was new and I'd failed Bram. I knew it, even if they didn't. Super-vamp powers came with super responsibility... or something like that. Admittedly, what I remembered most about *Spider-Man* was that upside-down kiss. Oh, and Toby Maguire's totally hot blue eyes.

But I wasn't thinking about that right then. I was thinking about kohl-lined chocolate brown eyes and how really awesome it would be to see them open.

"Bram?" I whispered.

His still-perfectly-shaped head didn't move.

"He's breathing on his own at least," Bella said in a hushed voice. "That's good."

I didn't know what it was about hospitals that made everybody—even me—speak in whispers.

Bella was right. An oxygen tube fed into Bram's nostrils, a heart monitor blipped away and an IV dripped, but he was breathing on his own. There was some kind of doohickey on one index finger that fed stats into yet another monitor, which beeped at intervals. It was a regular medical musical.

"Will he be okay?" I asked, turning to Officer Crinkly.

"That's for a doctor to say."

"But you know," I accused him. "You've talked to them."

He refused to say more, except to ask, "Do you want to see the other kids? The ones you put here?"

I shook my head. I'd had enough. The antiseptic smell of the hospital and the boop-boop of the equipment were overwhelming. It felt like my head might just explode.

None of the others wanted to see the bully boys either. Not surprising. I squeezed Bram's hand. Lily and Bella gave him a kiss on the forehead—very, very gently—and Ulric teased him about how unconscious guys got all the action. I almost smiled at that. I thought that if Bram were awake, he'd smile too.

7

We went quietly, but as soon as I hit the daylight, I knew I was in trouble. My skin started to burn and itch at the sting of the sun, and I realized that I hadn't had any of my fortified blood with its sunscreen potion since late last night. It shouldn't have been a problem. I'd gone longer without blood, but the whole awake-during-daylight thing apparently took more out of me than usual, and I hadn't been compensating. I hadn't even realized I needed to. Yet another thing to discuss with my keepers.

Ulric, seeing me wince, took it for emotion—or at least a good excuse to snake an arm around me. The flesh he touched, now shaded, nearly sang with relief.

"You okay?" he asked.

I gave him a sidelong glance. "*I'm* fine, but if *you* need a hug, knock yourself out."

"Really?"

"Hug only. Bust a move and you'll pull back a bloody stump. Capisce?" It wasn't until it was out of my mouth that I realized I was perfectly capable of making it happen. After what Ulric had seen, he probably realized it, too.

"I always knew you were trouble," he said, as though proud of it.

I smiled feebly and hurried to get to the car, out of the sun and his embrace that much sooner. Not that the hug felt bad. That was the problem. I was seriously in need of some distance. I was with Bobby. Ulric was an assignment, nothing more.

Lily's phone beeped at her as we got into the car, letting her know she'd missed a message at some point. She checked it as I pulled out.

"Gavin and Byron are fine. The police must have finished with them just before they came for us. They're hanging out at Gavin's place," she reported. "They want us to come by."

"I'm done in," I said, "but I'll drop you all there."

I was relieved, actually. One stop rather than three meant I could get to Agents Stick and Stuffed and my doctored blood that much the sooner. Get some answers, report on Rick's rage, maybe even feel Bobby's arms around me. I needed that in a way that my totally self-sufficient self didn't want to face.

Once the goth trio disappeared—into a remarkably normal looking whitewashed brick house—I drove like I was headed for a BOGO sale at Bloomies. Probably I should have driven in some kind of crazy, evasive pattern, just in case the police were tailing me or something, but the direct route meant I had a better chance of making it to Stick and Stuffed before I burst into flame. Already my eyeballs were on fire. Note to self: invest in some serious shades, maybe Dolce & Gabbana.

I called ahead to beg Agents S&S to raise the garage door for me so that I could drive right in, but it was Rick-the-rat who answered the phone, snarled at me, and hung up again. I was so relieved to see the doors slide upward at my approach, though, that I almost didn't want to hurt him.

As darkness closed in on me, I said an instinctive "Thank you, God!" even though I was pretty sure he'd blocked my calls when I went over to the dark side. I prepared to face Rick, who was glaring from the doorway of the house that he and Bobby shared with the Feds like one big, happy, dysfunctional family.

"We have to talk," I said, glaring back at him.

"Right," he sneered.

"No kidding," I continued. "*All* of us."

He called into the house, "Good thing you're all here.

Her royal highness has summoned us to an audience. All hail the royal slayer of innocents."

I brushed past him, accidentally swinging an elbow toward his solar plexus. All the air *ooph*ed out of him.

"First of all, I didn't *slay* anyone," I informed him. "And second, your guys were attacking *my* peeps, so don't even try playing the innocent card."

Three sets of eyes were staring at me as I entered the eat-in kitchen, which was right off the garage. Agent Stuffed had barricaded himself behind a wall of two laptops, a printer, and a stack of paperwork a mile high. Couldn't be much actual eating being done at that table, not without getting crumbs in the keyboard. Agent Stick poked her head out of the fridge to stare and then blink, shake her head, and stare again. But it was Bobby and his baby blues that really arrested my attention. He was looking at me like I'd just stepped out of a slasher film carrying a bloody chain saw.

"What?" I asked.

"You...you're kind of, um, *hot*," Bobby said, rising from his place at the table beside Agent Stuffed.

I blinked. "Well, duh, but—"

"No, I mean you're smokin', as in an actual fire hazard. And your skin is kind of, ah, peeling."

My hands flew up to my face, and I screamed. My skin felt like the outside of a fire-roasted marshmallow.

Agent Stick—Maya—shut the door of the fridge, grabbed a towel from the bar on the front of the stove, and took it to the sink to run cool water on before handing it to me. "Here, try this. I'll start you a cold shower."

Hands covering my deformity, I followed her out of the room. "Don't listen to a word Rick says before I get back!" I commanded.

Behind me I heard Rick laugh and vowed to kill him dead. Really dead. Like Rasputin's third-time's-the-charm level dead. Yeah, we'd heard all about Rasputin in spy school. He was the crazy Russian padre who'd advised the last czar and played faith-healer to his son. Assassins tried to take him down during the Russian Revolution. If only they'd staked him or cut off his head instead of poisoning, shooting, and drowning him, the Russians *still* might not know about vampires, and we wouldn't have had to waste so many spies and resources in that Cold War. The U.S. might even now be a true superpower, instead of just must-see TV for the rest of the world. Anyway, Rick was dead, dead, dead … as soon as I dealt with my really bad chemical peel.

"What happened?" Maya asked, running the water and unable to meet my eyes for long. I was that hideous.

"Too long in the sun. What the hell's going on with that? I used to only need blood every couple of days or so. Now … look, if I need more to keep from becoming a crispy critter, *you need to say so.*"

"Interesting," she answered.

"*Interesting?* Is that all you have to say?"

Now she met my eyes. "Look, the potion is experimental. Virtually hot off the presses. Possibly we have to refine—"

"So we're guinea pigs?" I...well, I didn't screech. I was brought up better than that.

"We've done some trials, of course," she said coolly, "but it was impossible to be sure of optimum dosages without a field test. So much depends on metabolism, exertion, exposure—"

"Great. Lovely. And, hey, if your test subjects burn up, it's instant cremation. No messy funeral costs, no covering up the body. Clean. Efficient. Probably even eco-friendly."

She didn't even blink. Just showed me to the towels and first aid supplies and let herself out.

Ten minutes later, I'd painfully scrubbed the charred skin from my face, and what was left was a newly grown, baby-fine layer so sensitive the very air hurt it. I couldn't imagine applying cream. Just like a peek-a-boo blouse, the new skin exposed veins and muscle, ligaments, whatever. I was totally hideous. I could only hope I'd dropped the others off *before* I'd reached the point of extra crispy.

I wrapped a towel around my body, bathhouse style, wrapped another around my head like a turban, and tried to keep my knees from buckling as I let myself back out into the hallway, pressing Maya's dishtowel to my face again to hide it from prying eyes.

"Got blood?" I asked as I hit the kitchen.

Bobby handed me a mug, pre-warmed, as I sat down beside him, totally without meeting his eyes.

"You're kind of, ah, under-dressed," he said. "But I like it."

"My clothes smell like barbecued me," I grumped. "Another set for the incinerator. At this rate, by Friday all I'll have left is my birthday suit."

"Excuse me?" Agent Stuffed asked.

"Never mind." I took a sip of the blood, which tasted like Ghirardelli hot chocolate to me right about then. A tingle shot all the way through me, part pain from the healing and part pleasure. I closed my eyes for a second to let the ripple of sensation pass. When I opened them again, everyone was staring.

"So, what shall we talk about first?" I asked. "The fact that the Feds are using us as lab rats for their daylight draught, Rick attacking me today at the hospital, or the weirdness at Red Rock?"

Bobby looked at Rick the way I looked at anyone standing between me and the last size six Manolo Blahniks in fire-engine red. "You attacked her?" he growled. "It *better* have been part of your cover."

Coming from Bobby, the Neanderthal thing was so … so totally sweet. It wasn't that I liked macho crap, it was just that I couldn't imagine Bobby pulling it for anyone but me.

"Whatever," Rick answered. "She started it."

"Me?" I asked, incredulous. "How exactly did *I* start it?"

"Children, don't make me separate you three," Agent Stick cut in, just like a real mom. "We've got bigger problems. Gina, we did some checking after you reported to Bobby yesterday. Read this."

Agent Stuffed—I was going to have to remember to think of him as Sid before I slipped up in his presence—passed us each a file, which I opened reluctantly, given that the last file had gotten me into all this. It was like a rap sheet on Red Rock. "The events you describe…" Agent…Sid…went on to summarize what was right there in front of us. "You talk about a power-boosted, out-of-control feeling—well, I researched the location, and Red Rock lies along the same ley line as your school. What's more, it's what we call a node. Think of it like a geyser—mostly quiet, but every once in a while it goes off, flares up, like it's doing now."

I looked at the dossier. As recently as thirty years ago, it had been the meeting place for some kind of coven. All fun and games, I guessed, until the leader was arrested for the negligent homicide of her own daughter, who'd gotten into her mother's spell supplies, some of which, like deadly nightshade, had earned their names. Red Rock had made it into the news. Way, way back before that, it had been sacred to the Hopewell Indians, a spot for special ceremonies calling on the Great Sky Father. Clearly a place of power.

"So it's flaring now?" I asked, shooting a quick glance at Rick. There had to be more to all this. Rick hadn't been at Red Rock last night with his new buddies. I'd have seen him.

Sid nodded.

"Our equipment still shows the disturbance centered around the school, but it could be radiating outward, activating other hot spots," Maya said.

"*Or*," Sid drew the word out, looking at each of us in turn, "the partying brought the place to life—libations poured with every drink spilled. Cuts, nicks, or other forms of bloodletting. Good way to wake a place of power."

"Good to know," I said, a lot more flippantly than I felt. I mean, sheesh, when I'd joked about using the force and turning to the dark side, I'd thought I was kidding. Now I had to watch out for *places* as well as people? And what did it mean that Red Rock had *my* blood? I'd walked around barefoot, cut my feet on rocks as I ran to Bella's aid.

"So, what do we do?" Bobby asked, ever practical.

"Stay away," Sid said fiercely. "Let it settle. Keep other kids away."

"Wow, way to be proactive," I mumbled.

Sid and Maya both glared.

"What does all this have to do with Rick?" I asked.

"I don't know," Sid admitted. "Rick?"

The man…boy…of the hour looked *pissed*. "How should I know? At lunch some of the guys and I were talking, and we just got more and more worked up, until Red and I decided to cut out, head over to the hospital—"

"Looking for a fight?" I asked.

"What? No! Just checking on our fallen, you know? And then I saw you and all this rage—" His fists clenched, vibrating with barely leashed fury.

We were all staring at him.

"What?" he asked again. "I didn't *do* anything. She's still…not breathing…isn't she?"

I stuck my tongue out at him in lieu of launching myself across the table, which in my current state of undress might not be the best idea ever.

"How do you feel now?" Sid asked.

Rick shrugged his tense shoulders. "I don't know. I don't exactly want to kill her, but I don't exactly *not* want to kill her."

"She has that effect on people," Sid muttered, getting me back for my earlier comment.

"Okay, onto the missing kids," Maya jumped in.

"I still want to talk about your *experimental* potion."

"There's nothing to talk about. You need more, you take more. End of story."

"Side effects?" I asked. "Potential for overdose? Will we build up a tolerance?"

"I guess we'll find out together," she answered with supreme unconcern. "Now, the missing kids." She tossed us each a stapled packet. "We've identified them as Tyler Dyson and Teresa Mendoza. Agent Epps and I are already watching the hospitals and morgues. We need you out among the kids. Find out if anyone's seen them and what rumors are circulating. They may even turn up. Gina, Teresa is apparently in your seventh-period art class, so you've probably met."

I shook my head. "I haven't even made it to seventh period yet. Yesterday was the party, today the hospital."

"Geez Louise," Sid groaned, running a hand down his face. If he'd been a cartoon, his features would have stretched and snapped comically back into place. Of course, if he were a cartoon, he'd probably still be in black and white. I mean, *Geez Louise*? What decade were we in anyway? "Why the hell did we go through all the trouble of arranging your classes to expose you to the most cliques if you're not even going to go?"

"Hey, I go where the investigation leads."

"Wild parties? Run-ins with the police?" he ranted.

"What're you—my father? The kids went missing from the party, didn't they? So I was in the right place, just—"

All the righteous indignation left me right about then, but I wasn't going to back down.

"Just looking the other way," Sid said, relentless. "Getting into trouble."

That hurt. Responsibility sucked rocks. Up until a few months ago, I hadn't been responsible for anything more than color-coordinating my wardrobe. But foil one vampire vixen bent on world domination and suddenly people expect all kinds of things. Some days it just didn't pay to wake up dead.

"*Fine*," I said through gritted teeth. "Bad secret agent. No cookie. So, what's the plan?"

"First, we get you dressed. I'm sure Maya will have something that fits."

"Damn," Bobby said under his breath. Maya shot him a disapproving look and I smiled.

"Then," Sid continued as if he hadn't spoken, "we hit the streets. Someone has to have seen something. We cover the hangouts, listen for the rumors. Maybe we'll catch a break and the kids will show up safe and sound. We ought to be about due for a break."

8

Rick and Maya got the mall. I'd think I was being pun-
ished, but as consolation prizes go, Bobby was a pretty
good one. He and I partnered up to hit the town's main
hangouts—the DQ, the Dunkin' Donuts, and the Denny's.
I kid you not. Until Sid listed them off, I had no idea we
had such a thing for the Ds. 'Course, it went along with the
other fave five D words I was starting to pick up hanging
with the goths—ditch, delinquent, dark, death, dreamy.
No, no, *dreary*, not dreamy. Lord, was I losing it?

We got to our first stop, the Dairy Queen, and I parked the tail end of my car with its *Dracula Is My Co-Pilot* bumper sticker up against a tree, just in case any of my crowd went cruising by—I'd told them I was done in. On the other hand, who hadn't had a sudden craving for a chocolate shake or goopy sundae at odd hours of the day or night? No one I knew. Of course, my mom, being totally figure-conscious, always took me for the low-fat, slow-churned kind with sugar-free fudge, hold the whipped cream, when we went at all. Good times. I tried not to think of her and Dad back in Ohio, still mourning my death. Or not mourning and turning my room into a home spa. It could go either way.

It wasn't hard to redirect my thoughts with Bobby sliding across the bench seat toward me.

"You know . . ." he said, trailing a couple of fingers over my thigh, which was clad in one of Maya's black skirts that, sadly, fell below the knee on me. It was still better than her pants, which would have flopped around my feet like clown shoes. "It's probable we'll be seen together. We need some kind of cover story."

"Oh, like you tutoring me in math?" I teased.

His fingers rose from my thigh to trace over my stomach, up the valley between my breasts. "Sure, like that," he answered. "Or anatomy or chemistry."

He leaned in for a kiss, and I met him halfway, nearly moaning at the contact. It had been way, way too long. Days.

I felt zippy like I had at Red Rock, only this time it was

all-natural. I slid my hands into his Zac-Efron-shaggy hair to hold him in place as I kissed him back. He stroked my hair, my neck, down again over my borrowed shirt. I started to shiver, trailing my hand down his chest, determined to get the same reaction out of him.

Something rocked the car, jolting us suddenly so that our teeth clicked together. We jumped, ready for action, and found that a pack of teens had decided to use my car instead of the nearby picnic tables for their snack. Two girls and a guy were planted on the hood, and three others stood peeking in our windows like we were the entertainment.

I glared back at the one staring in the driver's side window, hand up like a visor over his eyes to help him see inside. I debated slamming the horn, but I didn't think it would scatter them. Putting the car in drive... now *that* might do the trick.

"Rain check?" Bobby asked. "The sight of you in that towel was driving me nuts."

"Total rain check."

We shared a smoldering look and probably would have forgotten our audience and moved in for another lip-lock if the kissy sounds of the peeping Toms hadn't stopped us. The guy on my side had gone so far as to press his lips to my window and blow his cheeks out so that he looked like something out of *Wallace and Gromit*.

I turned the key, and hit the gas as the car rumbled to life so that it roared a *watch-out!* warning. The kids jumped back with a "Hey! What the—" like *I* was the one being unreasonable.

I put the car into drive and let it jump an inch to scare those who were slow to vacate the vicinity, but slammed on the breaks at what I saw just beyond them. It was Hailee, dressed in her signature red, but this time it was a hoodie with some kind of bedazzled design over the left side, and jeans tight enough that I could tell you the cut of her panties—if she were wearing any. She was walking with a guy who had a good six or seven inches on her.

But that wasn't what got me. He wasn't exactly a giant, not even to me at five foot nothing. And it wasn't even the fact that he was at an ice cream place without a smidge of frozen goodness, like the plain vanilla cone that Hailee was licking as she looked up seductively at him from beneath her lashes, a trick I could do with...okay, not with my eyes shut, but practically in my sleep. No, it was something else, but I couldn't quite figure out what it was.

Then my conscious caught up with my subconscious, which had always been the speed demon of the two.

"He's not breathing," I said aloud.

"Who isn't?" Bobby asked, eyeing the voyeurs we'd just chased off.

"Him," I said, pointing.

The guy had his arm around Hailee now and was steering her toward the wooded area behind the shop.

"The guy with Hailee?" he asked.

"Oh, so you're on a first-name basis with her?"

"You're jealous!" he said, one of those guy-grins spreading across his face. Smug so wasn't a good look for him.

"Do we have time for this?" I asked.

The smile vanished. "No."

We were out of the car, relinquishing it to the flock we'd just scattered, and halfway across the parking lot in the blink of an eye, but already the woods had swallowed Hailee and her undead date. There was a sharp contrast between the overgrown grass and the tree line, which was completely imposing. Tall trees, thickly grown. So much of Wappingers Falls, apart from Route 9, was like that—patches of civilization interspersed with woodlands that were probably unchanged since pre-pioneer days. Twigs snapped beneath our feet, and Bobby, leading the way, had to hold branches aside for me. We were far from stealthy, but the couple ahead of us didn't seem to notice. We came upon them not more than ten steps in, when Bobby stopped me with an upraised arm that I stood on my tiptoes to peer over.

They were locked in a clinch, only not the romancy kind. Instead of her lips, Hailee's escort was working on her neck. A trickle of blood escaped. While she looked like putty in his hands, I knew there was something to our bite that had that effect on our victims. It didn't necessarily signal consent.

"What should we do?" Bobby whispered.

Twigs snapped behind us—crack, crack, crack—and I turned to see the source. The kids I'd scared off the car had followed us.

"Hey!" one yelled, seeing they'd been spotted. "You nearly ran us down back there!"

As if. I looked back at Bobby. "You handle the mob. I've got Hailee." Because no way was I going to let him play her hero. Plus, he had particular powers that worked wicked well on mobs—mind control, telekinesis...

Bobby and I spun at vamp-speed, trading places so that I faced my baddy and he faced his, assuming it was one of *those* mobs—the kind with the run-you-over-to-get-the-last-dress-on-the-rack mentality.

My baddy seemed oblivious to it all, still sucking away on Hailee's neck. I didn't bother with a public service announcement of my presence, but sped into action, ready to peel the bloodsucker off the blond. Just as I was about to connect, he lashed out with an arm—lightning fast, even by vamp standards—and flung me clear.

I landed on my butt bone, shocked as hell. Behind me, Bobby cried out as well, but I had to trust him to look out for himself. I had problems of my own. My guy, the Fanged and the Furious, turned on me, letting Hailee fold like an end-of-season sales item. His eyes were so dark that even with my super senses, I couldn't tell the pupil from the rest. He had shark eyes. Charles Manson eyes. Deep and chaotic. He turned them on me with terrifying intensity, as if trying to will me away. Sure enough, I heard *Begone* in my head, with a mental push for good measure—which was a good thing, because it was so heavily accented I wouldn't have gotten the meaning otherwise. I snorted. It was all so B-movie sounding, like he was going for Transylvanian.

"*Whatever*," I said out loud. "That's not the way I roll. You want me gone, you're going to have to do it yourself."

His eyes widened, then he hissed and came at me, his hands curved into claws and his teeth gleaming wetly in the little moonlight that streamed through the tree canopy. I struggled to stand up, but I wasn't going to make it in time. I settled for launching myself ungracefully aside. I did a quick mental check of my arsenal, but I hadn't come prepared for vampire slayage—I didn't normally carry around the means of my own death.

The car keys were still in my hand from the mad dash across the field, but they wouldn't do much good unless I could pierce a major artery or something... Damn, if only Bobby and I'd had more time for anatomy lessons.

I shot to my feet as Fanged and Furious blew past me, and was ready when he whirled again. We eyed each other. He snarled like a pissed-off pit bull, and we clashed—hands clenching hands, him snapping at me with his bloodstained teeth. We looked to be locked in some twisted tango. I instinctively raised a knee to give him a what-for, but it didn't even phase him, so I head-butted his mouth as he came for me again. The advantage of being small was that he had to bend to go for my soft spots, and I'd always been hard-headed.

He reared back, and I took the opportunity to jab my keys into his neck. Blood spurted, and a newer, ickier instinct had me catching it on my tongue. My eyelids flickered shut for a second in ecstasy, and when I opened them again, he was gone—the crash of the branches and the snapping twigs the only evidence of his path.

I turned to check on Bobby, to decide whether I should go after F&F or help him out, and saw Bobby laying low his last opponent—physically. I'd expected him to use his Jedi mind-tricks and convince them we weren't the droids they were looking for or whatever … yes, he'd made me watch the *Star Wars* saga with him, twice … if it weren't for the hotness of Han Solo … But instead, Bobby'd chosen the physical approach.

Anyway, he didn't need me. I took off after Fanged and Furious, but I couldn't hear his crashing over my own, and it didn't take me long to realize that as a tracker, I was a bust. Boy Scout Bobby would probably have done a lot better, but when I headed back toward him, I saw he was too busy with a handful of Hailee. One arm supported her while the other hand gently brushed the hair back from her face and neck to check out the bite marks. She was fully aware, eying him like something she'd enjoy a helluva lot more than her namby-pamby vanilla cone.

Bobby saw me in the trees, and I signaled that I was going back to the car. There was no need for Hailee to see us together, as much as I wanted to stake my claim to Bobby right then and there.

I realized, as I approached the car, that I'd have to clean off my keys before I could use them in the lock. I hated to waste good blood, but I was out of the treeline now and had no choice but to wipe them on Maya's skirt. The blood stains would come out, or they wouldn't. I tried not to worry about things beyond my control.

As I wiped the keys down and let myself into the car, Bobby's mind-speak came through loud and clear. *You okay?*

I collapsed onto my seat and closed the door, as if that

were necessary for a private conversation. *What the hell happened back there? Did you have to take people down like that?*

I hadn't meant to start with accusations, but the aggression I'd seen was so out of character for Bobby. And after Rick…

Something was messing with my mental mojo, he answered. *I couldn't reach them. It was like when Internet access is down and you can't even connect with the server.*

Well, that was new and disturbing. Even if Bobby couldn't control me—I had some kind of mental block when it came to doing what others wanted—he could connect with me. So either these kids, all of them, had blocking powers that were a step beyond me, which I refused to even consider, or there was something else going on here. Maybe it had to do with the weirdness of the ley lines or whatever was causing the spontaneous freakouts… But whatever it was, without Bobby's mega magic…

But you reached me, I said back.

This time, he answered. *But I tried to talk to you in the woods when I was seeing to Hailee.*

Oh, right. Hailee was hurt. I was supposed to be caring. *How is she?*

Weak. She's lost a lot of blood. I've called 911 from the cell phone of one of the downed guys. If my mojo's back in working order, I'll give everyone memories that don't include us. Take the car to the gas station down the street. I'll meet you there as soon as the EMTs arrive. I want to watch over everyone until then in case that vampire guy comes back.

Made sense. That way, if the cops came with the EMTs we wouldn't be caught up in the questioning. Plus, Hailee wouldn't remember her hero-worship of *my* honey. It was a win-win.

Do you think you can track him? I asked. *I mean, does your magic have an ap for that?*

Somehow he managed to convey humor through the mind-link. *I don't think so.*

Well darn.

I moved the car and called Agent Stuffed ... Sid, *Sid.* How long was it going to take me to get that and make it stick? I reported in.

He was silent for a second. Then, "So now we've got flaring ley lines, missing kids, and *vampires?*"

"Oh my," I agreed.

9

I couldn't believe we had to go to stupid school when there were leads to chase down, vampires to vanquish, and all that crap. But here I was, sitting in homeroom, paying tribute to the all-important attendance.

"Geneva Belfry," Mr. Richardson called.

"Yo," I answered.

He looked like he wanted to say that "Here" would be much more appropriate, but I'd worn him down already and he moved on, leaving me to my thoughts.

The story of the weird attack at the DQ last night was the talk of the school. Kids speculated, like the reporters on the morning news, about what connection the trouble might have with the missing twosome. No one had any answers.

Attendance didn't take long this morning since the school was practically a ghost town now. Parents were keeping their kids home because of all the trouble, or maybe it was just another symptom of the insanity. Stick and Stuffed had mentioned falling attendance and sleepwalking through school. I could easily believe it. Even Mr. Richardson was so low-key today he didn't even *try* to keep us from talking through the announcements.

I dragged my feet on the way to my locker until I saw that Ulric was waiting for me. If he proposed another skip day, I was so there. Math and science and all that jazz just weren't going to cut it today.

But his face didn't hold any mischief. It kind of looked like a Johnny Depp face in a Tim Burton film. You know the one—serious, maybe a little unhinged.

"Hear you had a date last night," he said in greeting. "That why you ditched us?"

I halted, honestly baffled for a second. "Oh, *that*," I answered when the light bulb went on in my head. "That wasn't a date."

As secretive as we'd tried to be, someone must have seen Bobby and me at the Dairy Queen. But Ulric wasn't owed any explanation, and the kinda-flattering attention he'd been paying me so far was going to wear thin if he started getting all territorial.

"Reeaally?"

"Yup," I answered, twisting in my locker code and ignoring him as best I could.

"I heard you were out with some geek. Same place as the trouble last night. Weird, huh?"

I shoved half the books in my backpack into the locker and slammed it shut with extreme prejudice before I whirled on him. "What exactly are you accusing me of? Eating in a public place? Oh, the horror. Newsflash, I plan to do it again this afternoon. Fifth period, in fact. High school cafeteria. Imagine the scandal."

I started to walk away, thinking it was a pretty good exit line, but Ulric grabbed me by the shoulder. I looked at his hand like I could wither it, which, of course, I couldn't.

"Wait, I'm ... sorry." He sounded as surprised as I felt.

"You should be," I told him.

"I don't know what got into me. I just ... Here, let me make it up to you. Tonight. Battle of the Bands. Bella's performing and we're all going to root her on. It'll be my treat."

"Did you really just use your stalker-boy come-on to ask me out on a date?"

He actually had the good grace to look embarrassed. "If I say yes, do I get points for honesty?"

I didn't have to think hard about the answer to that one, but I couldn't exactly say what was on my mind. Spy stuff was sneaky that way.

"I'll tell you what," I said instead. "I'll go. You can pay for my ticket as an apology. But it's not a date."

A grin started twitching his lips upward. And here I'd thought goths were supposed to be all eternal gloom and doom. I wasn't sure he'd quite gotten the memo.

"Sure. Not a date. I'll pick you up at six thirty."

Before I could protest about my own wheels or his lack of my address, he was gone, disappeared as if he never was. And in the half-empty hallway, that was a pretty good feat. Damn him. I might just have to move him from the mental file of "obnoxious but good for the ego" to "intense and potentially stalkerific."

•   •   •

When 6:35 rolled around with no sign of stalkerboy, I was tempted to take off in my own car. I was debating whether or not to leave a note when Ulric pulled up in a black Sebring ragtop. There was someone with him.

Two guys unfurled themselves from the front seats, then Byron started to let himself into the back.

"Where's the hearse?" I asked.

"Blew a gasket," Byron answered, all morose.

"Sure you don't mean blew a casket?" I asked.

They both stared at me. "Okay, I admit it. That was lame."

"Really lame," Byron agreed. "I'm surprised Ulric didn't think of it first."

Ulric punched him in the arm and came around the passenger side to hold the door open for me.

"Not a date," I reminded him as I got in.

"My apology for being late," he said. "Of course, that was really Byron's fault. If he hadn't needed a ride..."

"Fine," Byron said, "it's all my fault. Can we get going?"

I rolled my eyes and tucked myself into the car. I'd been careful not to wear a skirt tonight, lest Ulric take it for a come-on, but I couldn't resist the cool jeans I'd found among the other basic-black denim in my wardrobe. These had mesh where the side-seams should be and were kind of sexy without being actually slutty. Not that I minded slutty particularly, but Ulric totally didn't need the encouragement. I'd paired it with a black mesh shirt over a red tank top. My long dark hair was twisted into two buns on top of my head, held there with chopsticks. I figured that if the vamp from the DQ came calling, I'd have ready-made stakes at my disposal this time. Plus, I was the ultimate in goth chic... as long as I didn't trip and impale myself.

The auditorium parking lot, way down the long arm of the L, was full when we got there, so we had to park out in the boondocks by the center of the school. The guys didn't know how lucky they were to have a hot, kick-butt vampire chick to watch their backs. Of course, Ulric would have preferred to watch mine and tried that "after you" trick, but I told him I'd rather keep him in my sights.

Byron made a choking sound that I thought was probably a laugh.

"Wow, tough crowd," Ulric groused.

"You have no idea," I told him.

Inside, the place was swarming. The bands hadn't started yet, so even though the auditorium doors were wide open for people to take their seats, folks were still milling around in the lobby. Some were in line for tickets at the small box office—no more than a closet, really, with a roll-up window. Most were making a run on the bake sale table.

I spotted Lily right away, holding up a wall as she kept an eye on the new arrivals. It was pretty hard to miss her, actually, in her sheath dress of toxic-waste green with black-and-white-striped stockings and matching gloves. Her baby-fine hair was pulled into a ponytail that was practically on top of her head and teased to within an inch of its life.

I left the guys immediately to hang with her, but, of course, they followed.

"Hey, you dressed up," I said.

She shrugged. "I wanted Bella to see me cheering."

"Shouldn't be a problem."

Lily looked behind me to my escorts. "Where's Gavin?"

"It wasn't my day to watch him," Ulric said.

Lily looked disappointed. "Well, shall we?" she asked, cocking her head toward the open auditorium doors off to her left.

"Just a minute, we have to get our tick—"

I didn't even get to finish my sentence before Ulric was flashing two tickets at me. "I stopped at lunch. Figured it would save time."

They started flashing the lights in the lobby to let us know it was time to take our seats inside. We went in and were lucky enough to find seats all together, two-thirds of the way back in the auditorium. It wasn't completely full, but there was a pretty respectable audience.

"Bella's band is up fourth," Lily whispered. "Just before the break."

But first we had to get through a really, really awful punk band that made Rage Against the Latrine seem like musical genius, a girl who didn't quite understand the concept of "band" and accompanied herself on guitar as she sang—not too badly, actually—and a group that played Latin music. It wasn't really my thing, but the singer's eyes were smoldering and he had a pretty fair idea of how to shake those hips…Ulric bumped my knee at a certain point, though I knew I hadn't been drooling. Like he had any moral high ground here anyway, after he'd brought a third wheel on our non-date.

Bella's band appeared before she did, three guys dressed in abstract-patterned T-shirts of gray and black over jeans. One keyboardist and two guitarists—one probably a bassist (I could never tell the diff). It was only after they'd fussed with their equipment that Bella practically floated out, which made sense, because she couldn't weigh more than a feather. The stage lights made her silver slip dress glow and sparked off her dark flowing hair. They washed out her ever-pale face until it was just an impression of big, kohl-lined eyes and red lips. Her bruise from the jerky boys at Red Rock was nowhere to be seen, probably buried under a gallon of concealer. She grabbed the microphone in one hand, half shut her eyes as if tuning us out, and retreated behind her lids. She started to sing even before her musical accompaniment began.

The sound was high, pure, and haunting, like Evanescence. She sang like some supernatural being—an angel or a siren or something unearthly. The instruments, when they joined in, were just distracting at first, but took on more of a duet role as they went on, weaving in and out of her sound rather than merging with it.

I realized I'd actually forgotten to breathe for at least a few beats. I hoped no one noticed, but looking left and right, I didn't have to worry. No one was paying *me* any attention at all.

When Bella's last note died, the audience erupted in a fit of clapping and wolf calls. Lily not only stood up, she jumped up on her chair and waved her arms, screaming her enthusiasm. I saw Bella give a small smile as she spotted Lily. Then she was gone, and I gave Lily a hand down.

"Wow," I said. "That was incredible."

"I *know*! Let's go tell her."

We shooed the guys out of the row, but not before the rest of the crowd had poured into the aisles for intermission. It took us a while to make our way to the hallway leading backstage, which had been blocked off with sawhorses. There was a straightlaced guy manning them who was explaining to those who'd gotten there before us that he couldn't let anyone back there except the bands.

"What, paparazzi a problem?" I asked, a little too loudly.

He zeroed in on me over the heads of the others. "No, theft. A lot of equipment back here. It's an insurance thing."

"Darn, 'cause I sure could use me a snare drum." Not that I had any clue how to tell a snare drum from any other.

Lily gave me a *look*, and as the other students reared back to stare at me she used the path created to sidle up to the enforcer.

"Can you just get a message to our friend?" she asked, batting her lashes up at him.

"Can't leave my post, but if you tell me her name, I can try to get someone to call her for you and you can tell her yourself."

"Belladonna. She was the last to play."

Rule Guy's lips twisted. "Like I even had to ask. Anyway, you missed her. She left. Said she'd be back soon."

Lily shot me a despairing look over her shoulder, and I wondered if poor Bella ever got to use the facilities without people thinking the worst.

"Split up," she said.

"You want to hunt her down?" I asked.

"Did you see her swaying on stage? I doubt she ate anything before going on tonight. Maybe we should swing by the bake sale table and pick something up for her."

And here I'd thought all that swaying was musically inspired.

I nodded, and we took off at a speedwalk. Goths didn't run, I figured.

"She prone to passing out?" I asked.

"Once or twice." We still had our tail. "Byron, Ulric,

make yourselves useful," Lily snapped. "Start looking. Call me if you find her."

They peeled off without protest. Good to know Ulric could take orders. Maybe he wasn't a total loss.

There was no sign of Bella at the bake sale table. I grabbed a couple of cookies, threw down a dollar without waiting for anyone to collect, and took off toward the hallway that led to the rest of the school. The only other place to search was the area surrounding the auditorium and outdoors. I left that to Lily. If Bella was in bad shape, either through lack of food or gorging herself on baked goods at intermission and feeling the need to purge, she'd probably want to be as far away from witnesses as possible. I would.

For some reason, Lily's urgency had really gotten to me. With Bella separated from the pack, there was no telling what kind of trouble she could get into. A vamp was stalking the town—attacking at least one student that we knew of—and students were prone to going on the rampage.

The door between the auditorium area and the main part of the school was locked. Or, at least, the push bar didn't want to budge when I pressed on it. I took a few steps back and really launched myself at it, and the door popped open like maybe it had just been stuck. I looked around to see if the noise had attracted any attention, but no one was in my part of the hallway, and anyway I didn't know why I was being so paranoid. Something had me jumpy. My very nerves seemed to quiver with some kind of anticipation.

I went through the door, easing it shut behind me, and crept through the eerily dark hallway until I heard voices. Even with my super-vamp hearing, I couldn't separate the noise into words. It sounded like the adults from Charlie Brown "wah-wh-wahing" their way through a conversation, but I could get closer.

I traced the convo to a classroom around the next corner, in the science wing, and snuck up to the door. *If only I could see through walls*, I thought. But I couldn't, so I was going to have to pop my head into full view of the window so that I could peek into the room.

Slowly, I eased into viewing range. The room was dark, lit only by some outside light source that wasn't close enough to give it more than a glow, though it was enough for my vamp-o-vision. Inside, the place was deserted except for lab tables, chairs, and a single figure facing away from the door—tall, medium build, tousled hair, fists pressing the black leather jacket he was wearing to his hips. No, not a single figure. Make that two, because he was talking to someone he was blocking from view.

"It's not *working*," the someone said. I had to strain to hear until that last word, which carried all the frustration of something said more than once to no effect. "*I* got attacked, for God's sake. And they—"

Attacked? Who? The voice was definitely feminine, but I couldn't pick out more than that. It could be Hailee or Bella or even the missing girl, Teresa. I *had* to get a better look.

"I had nothing to do with that," the man said, waving a hand to brush away her concern.

"But your people—"

"Are no business of yours. I will deal with them. You know what you have to do. Trust me, you don't want to go back on our understanding." His voice dripped with menace, and the smallest hint of both an accent and a lisp. I suddenly had a chilling sense of who "his people" were...the same fanged fraternity that had granted me eternal unlife and the occasional speech impediment.

So it looked like there was more than one vampire running around town. Because this guy wasn't the one who'd attacked Hailee. The hair was all wrong, though the accent was close, if a lot less obvious.

"But I've just told you, you need to fix the formula," the girl said. "People are going haywire, the ones who don't just bring their own. Hell, half of them are dropping out."

Huh?

There was a second of silence. "Do not presume to tell me what to do...to tell *the council* what needs to be done."

Oh crap, the council? As in the vampire council that hated Bobby's and my guts and tried back in Ohio to kill the lot of us? Crap, crap, crap on a cracker.

"I'm sorry, I..." The girl started to back away, almost to the point where I could see her. Just a little more to the left, and—

"What are you doing?" Ulric's voice hissed in my ear.

I jumped right out of my skin, knocking against the door and making it rattle in its frame.

"Crap!" I cried, and not quietly, since stealth had gone right out the window.

"What was that?" the man said, and before I could curse Ulric or send him away from danger—it was a toss-up as to which way I'd jump—the door was yanked open and I was face-to-face with Kurt Cobain's evil twin. Somehow, even though I knew it wasn't a rule, it always surprised me when vamps weren't tall, *dark*, and deadly. They really shouldn't look like surfer boys or grunge musicians. I'm just saying.

"You!" he said, pupils huge and veins popping around them. His fangs were out in full force and behind me, Ulric gasped. It was the weirdest reaction … Grunge Vamp's, not Ulric's. I knew I'd never seen this guy before—I'd have remembered. So why was he "You!"ing me like we were old enemies?

"Sorry, I don't think we've been intro—"

Lightning fast, he grabbed my arm and made as if to pull me into the room, but I grabbed the doorjamb and yanked with all my might. It shocked him that little ole me was able to unbalance him. It was leverage, pure and simple, since we both had supersonic reflexes and he had, like, a foot on me. But he was shocked enough that I was able to pull him straight into the hallway and apply a boot to his butt as I released his arm. That and the momentum sent him flying at the opposite wall.

"Run!" I ordered Ulric.

"Like hell," he answered, proving that boys could never be trusted to listen when it messed with their machismo.

Grunge Vamp's accomplice didn't emerge from the room to check on him, so I doubled back to see who it was. But something hit me, and I went down before I could so much as think "tackle" or "unnecessary roughness." My face was mashed against cold tile that smelled of bleach, and the grease monkey on my back seemed to weigh two hundred pounds.

"*Get off her!*" Ulric yelled. The pressure on me only increased as Ulric made some kind of attack, but Grunge snarled and lashed out at him, shifting his weight enough for me to roll and buck, knocking him to the side. One of his legs still pinned me, but I shot up from the waist, leading with the heel of my hand, ready to jam his nose up into his cranial cavity. He flinched away and I struck his cheek, but not hard enough to do any real damage. I had a flash of Ulric lying like a rag doll where he'd been thrown down, but I caught him looking, like he was playing possum, waiting for another chance to attack. I shook my head subtly but had no faith he'd listen, and no time for anything else as Grunge launched himself at me again, totally telegraphing that he was going for my throat by the curl of his fingers, as if he could already feel it.

I grabbed the hair sticks out of my bun and blocked him with my other arm as I aimed them straight at his chest...as best I could with my hair falling down around me. Grunge screamed like a little girl as my stake struck. He convulsed around it, protecting his heart—which I seemed to have missed, because the ruby red eyes that met mine were filled with much more fury than surprise or despair.

"You're dead meat," he snarled.

He pulled something out of a pocket and threw it to the floor. Thick black smoke rose up, blinding me, stinging my eyes. And his eyes, I'd imagine, but he'd known it was coming and must have blinked, because suddenly he was gone and I couldn't even see anything to chase.

Ulric sounded like he was hacking up a lung. I blindly felt my way over to him, pretty grateful I didn't have to breathe this stuff in.

"Anything broken?" I asked.

"No," he coughed, which was followed by the automatic-weapons-fire staccato of even more coughing.

"Good. Stay put."

The smoke was clearing...or at least I thought so, because I was starting to get vague impressions of things through the red haze. I stumbled toward the open classroom, arms out in front of me, and looked inside. If the girl that Grunge had been talking to was still there, she wasn't out in the open.

"You might as well come out," I called, stepping inside and closing the door behind me to discourage escape, only realizing as it clicked shut that I'd just made myself a helluva target. Whoever was—had been?—in this room would have been sheltered from that smoke bomb and could probably still see. The room was deathly quiet, though. Not a creature was stirring—not even a lab mouse.

"I'll find you," I said, wiping away my bloody tears and starting my slow search around the room. Things were becoming clearer as my vamp healing went into overdrive, but it didn't do me any good...the room was empty.

I cursed and went back out to Ulric, who'd propped himself up against the wall and was trying to use the base of his T-shirt to wipe away tears and—eww!—snot. Bobby, never a slouch to begin with, was looking better every second. When Ulric spotted me, his bloodshot eyes widened.

"Whoa, what are you? Some kind of Chosen? Like Buffy the Vampire Slayer? Those were some *sick* moves. You and that guy were going so fast I could hardly even see you."

I flinched, but only on the inside.

"Tae kwon do," I lied. "I'm a black belt."

Ulric got to his feet, still blinking away the effects of the smoke bomb. "Yeah right. I took karate for a while when I was ten. I know what martial arts look like, and I've never seen anything like that."

"You must have been doing it wrong," I said. "But I'm sure you looked cute in your little uniform." In my experience, the word "cute" was pretty much guaranteed to distract anyone with a Y chromosome into an argument, but Ulric held his ground.

"I know what I saw."

"You just said we were moving too fast for you to see anything. Anyway, unless you want to be talking to some school shrink or worse, I'd keep your theories to yourself."

His nose was still running, and he sniffled noisily. "Too late. The rumors started right after Red Rock. Not me!" he said defensively, as I gave him the death glare of doom. "But, babe, I knew you for fierce the first second I saw you, and damn, you don't disappoint."

"Then you'd better fear me, sniffles. You keep this

quiet and don't *ever* call me babe. That's a name for Disneyfied pigs, not booty-kicking Bettys, got me?"

"Jeez, whatever." He rolled his eyes. "You don't think much of yourself, do you?"

Ulric's cell phone suddenly blared some heavy metal tune, almost making me jump and totally sending my comeback right out of my head. He grabbed the cell out of his pocket. "Yeah?"

I could tell from the sudden easing of his body posture that it was good news.

"Cool, we're on our way back," he reported.

He snapped the phone shut and told me, "They found Bella... or anyway, *she* found them. It's all good."

"Where was she?"

"Don't know," he answered. "You can ask her yourself when you see her."

We started walking back the way we'd come, but Ulric was moving with a limp. His mouth was screwed up, like he was in pain but trying to be manly about the whole thing.

"Aw, crap. Put your arm around me," I ordered. "I'll help you along."

"I knew you wanted me," he said, grimace mutating into a twisted grin.

I snorted. "Hardly. Use this to cop a feel and I drop you on your ass," I promised him.

• • •

I was far too beat to make my way over to the Fed family's faux-happy home for a face-to-face debriefing. Potion or no, being up and at 'em during daylight hours was hell on a vamp body. I felt like I'd been partying at a weeklong rave, only without all the fun. Well, okay, kicking Grunge Vamp's butt had been kind of a treat, but my cover already had more holes in it than Courtney Love's head.

So, I insisted Ulric and I cut out early from the Battle of the Bands. I'm sure the others thought we were going to make out, or that maybe I'd be playing doctor with him and his bad leg. Byron even offered to find his own way home. But the truth was, I wanted the privacy of my place to make a call, and I wanted Ulric out of the social scene as soon as possible to limit his urge to talk about what he'd witnessed.

His leg must really have been hurting, because he didn't even try for a good-night kiss, though he did tell me I was one wild ride and he'd see me around. Thank God it was Friday and I had a weekend to come up with better stories than I'd been throwing out so far.

Once inside, I threw the locks, checked the windows, and sat down to speed-dial Bobby. Maya answered instead.

"There was a vampire at the school tonight. He seemed to know me," I said without even a "hello."

There was dead silence on the other end for a minute, then, "That's bad."

I rolled my eyes, but she couldn't see it. "Thanks for the news flash. Any theories?"

Again that pause, and I knew Agent Stick knew something and was debating what to tell me.

"The vampire council has issued a KOC on you and Bobby."

"Knights of Columbus?" I asked, baffled.

She sighed heavily into the phone. "Kill or Capture. Dead or Alive. You get the picture. If that vamp recognized you ... well, it can't be long before the council knows you're here. Anyone who brings you in would score major points ... not to mention a reward."

"Bobby and I can't be the only ones they want. All of smelly Melli's minions—your entire team—"

"Yes, but you and Bobby are *special*, remember?"

Oh crap. I went cold inside. "Special" was supposed to be a good thing, but with Bobby sporting major mojo and me resistant to their mind games—well, I guess it made us irresistible to vamps and Feds alike. And with both sides, if you weren't for them, you were against. I knew what the vamp council did with liabilities. I didn't suppose the Feds were any less ruthless.

As if my heart could still clench, my whole chest went tight and I couldn't seem to draw enough breath for my next words.

"I've got some names for you to check out," I said, hoping to prove myself too useful to stake. "Belladonna Rigby, Hailee Johnson, and any other girl who's been attacked recently. Some girl is working with the vamps and seemed pretty upset she'd been victimized herself. I didn't get a good look." Or any at all.

"That would have helped," she said tightly.

"Hey, but good work on the rest of it," I said for her.

"Yeah, that," she agreed dryly. "You need to come in and look at our vamp database. See if you can ID the ones you've seen."

My brows drew together despite my best efforts, but then again, I no longer had to worry about wrinkles. "Huh? How'd you get vampire mug shots? We don't show on film."

"Same way the council put your picture out on their KOC order—sketch artists."

Now that she'd said it, it seemed perfectly obvious, but the thought of going anywhere tonight … my body seemed to be shutting down, that coldness in my chest just the start. Suddenly it was as if my body's kill switch had just been hit. I shuddered at the thought, but it was more of a quiver, like my body didn't have the resources for any stronger reaction.

"Can't make it anywhere tonight," I managed, my voice growing thick with the exhaustion. My tongue seemed to weigh twenty pounds all by itself and the rest of me felt like it was made of lead. I wasn't even sure I'd make it into the bedroom to sleep. If I could spare the energy, I'd have been terrified to be so vulnerable, with the vamps and maybe the Feds gunning for me. As it was …

"Gina, you okay?" Maya actually sounded concerned, but I couldn't be certain because I was hearing her from a long, long way away. My neck no longer seemed able to hold my head up and my fingers wouldn't grasp the phone, which slid to the floor. Probably I should have chugged blood when I first got through the door, but it was too late for that now. My body slipped into a heap on the floor, brain confused by the sudden slip-slide of images, and I knew there was something I should be remembering. Something… but I couldn't think of it before it was lights out.

10

I woke up to Maya standing over me. I bolted straight upright in my bed, wondering how I got there, only to nearly lay myself back down with dizziness. I needed a transfusion... stat.

"Get up," she ordered.

I hated to admit weakness, but I didn't see any way around it. And anyway, she could have killed me in my sleep if she'd really wanted to. "Don't think I can," I admitted. The room was starting to get fuzzy around the edges.

She handed me one of the To-Go bottles of blood from my refrigerator—still cold. No warm-up for exposed agents. No one who hasn't drunk cold, thick, gelatinous blood straight-up can have any idea the sheer horror of it. No reality show has ever come up with a challenge so terrible, I promise you. But I was a survivor. Moving at human speed, I grabbed the bottle, struggled with the top, and closed my eyes. Maybe I could fool myself into thinking this was gazpacho or chilled strawberry soup. Mmm... gak! My brain wasn't accepting the substitution. I choked the blood down as best I could and felt energy flowing into my limbs, breaking the ice that had settled in my core.

Maya grabbed another bottle of blood for the road and said, "Come on. Up now."

Wow, her bedside manner was touching.

"Where?" I asked. Just because she hadn't killed me yet didn't mean she wasn't going to. Maybe she wanted to debrief me first. Maybe she'd use me as a bargaining chip with the vamps—turn me over in exchange for them pulling out of Wappingers or handing over the Feds' fanged most wanted.

"Home base. Vampire mug shots. Plus, we want to go over what you heard and saw in detail."

Oh joy. I chugged the last bit of my cold, horrible meal and tried to suppress my gag reflex. I needed my energy for whatever the Feds might throw at me.

"Come on," she repeated, reaching to help me along.

"Can I change first? Shower?"

She was shaking her head. "No time... but you can run

a brush through that hair…and for God's sake, brush your teeth."

I smiled at that, imagining them stained red and hoping she was secretly a little freaked, but she just returned an eerily evil smile and pushed me toward the bathroom.

I locked the door behind me and took ten full minutes anyway to run a quick washcloth over myself and right my makeup. Falling asleep in mascara—so not recommended for the living. Oh sure, the bride of Frankenstein could get away with it, but she had all that crazy hair as a distraction. I also took a sec to call out to Bobby with my mind.

Bobby! I shouted, wanting to be really sure before I opened that bathroom door that death wasn't waiting for me on the other side.

All was ominously silent.

Maya pounded on the door. "Gina, your time is up!" I hoped she didn't mean that literally. "Let's go!"

I grimaced at my non-existent reflection in the mirror and went to meet my doom.

The car ride over to the mom-and-pop house was silent, except for me gulping at the cold blood and doing my best to bypass my taste buds. Light was barely teasing at the horizon. I thought a million times about asking if I was dead meat, but it wasn't like she'd tell me anyway. My only consolation was that if I was compromised, so, probably, was Bobby and they wouldn't want to lose him and his special powers—no way, no how. They'd find a way to salvage things. And while I didn't have any wicked mojo of my own, there was that resistance to other vamps' mind control, and a psycho-psychic just months ago had told me that I was *chaos*. Hear me roar. I had no idea whether he meant it in the supernatural way or if he was just commenting on my personality, but unlife sure had been a roller-coaster ride so far.

By the time we reached the house and slid the car into the garage, I was feeling much better. Maybe it was the blood, maybe it was my personal pep talk, but I had it in me to give the car door a nice, hearty slam to announce my presence, hopefully to Bobby, and strut in after Maya.

The sight of Sid sitting just where I'd left him—at the table, surrounded by computers and printouts, a jumbo mug of coffee at his elbow—was reassuring. Bobby sat just two seats away, a pile of school books in front of him.

"I *called* you this morning," I told him. It came out all accusatory, like he'd deliberately ignored me. I half-knew it was unreasonable, but the other half of me thought that as my vampire sire, if not as my boyfriend, he should have *known* I needed him.

"Sorry. I've been kind of focused. Getting a start on all this homework."

"But it's Saturday morning!"

"Sure. If I get it all done now I have the whole week-end ahead of me."

"Or you can relax a little and do it all Sunday night when you're fresh."

He looked at me like I'd lost my marbles. "What if an emergency comes up and I haven't done it. Then I'm SOL."

If he hadn't used "SOL," I'd have been absolutely convinced he was some kind of manbot masquerading as a teenaged boy. Who worried about homework in the event of an emergency?

"Children," Maya snapped, "can we get down to business?"

Oh sure, for *this* Bobby pushed his books aside.

I sat down across from him and proceeded to tell them everything. Midway through, Rick wandered in, carrying a cold, sweating can of Coke. Maya gave him a *mom* look for his tardiness, but no one interrupted my report. Next it was Sid's turn.

"Going on what you said, I did a check of girls from school who'd been attacked recently. I came up with three. First, Hailee Johnson, head cheerleader, solid B student. Mother is a pharmacist, father a computer consultant, currently out of work. No unusual notes in her school records, no police file. Nothing to label her a troublemaker. The only thing I turned up is that her line traces back to one of the women convicted in the Salem witch trials."

"You did her genealogy?" Rick asked, nearly snarfing Coke.

"I read her Facebook page," Sid answered, so deadpan that I figured it for the truth.

"But I thought the women killed in the witch trials were all innocents," Bobby cut in. "And that the mass hysteria was traced back to rye gone bad, some kind of hallucinogenic mold." It was kind of cool, in a totally geeky way, that he could pull stuff like that right out of his ass.

Sid looked impressed and irritated all at once. "I never

said her ancestor was killed. I said *convicted*. She escaped. The guilty ones generally did."

We all digested that for a second. It was a great story. I'd rent the DVD. Bobby would probably read the book.

"Next we have Belladonna Rigby. Also a senior. C student. Her only extracurricular activities seem to be her band and partying. Many notations in her file, mostly tardies, skips, and clinic notes about passing out in class and a possible eating disorder."

"Bulimia," I said. "Her friends are all worried."

Sid looked at me for a second.

"Well, we—they—are," I added defensively.

"*Anyway*, her mother sells Avon out of the house and takes care of her little brother, and her father runs a food service. The same one that supplies the school."

That perked us up, but he held up a hand to keep us from commenting.

"The third suspect is Marissa Muldoon, a junior who was roughed up in the locker room last week by a gang of other girls who said she looked at them funny. Artsy girl. Big into photography electives. Mother is a real estate agent. Father not in the picture. Last year when he had her for the weekend, they were in a serious car accident that left Marissa with whiplash and nerve damage to her face. The whiplash got better, but the nerve damage, not so much. No reason to suspect she's part of this, unless she's in league with the vamps for some supernatural healing."

"What about Teresa?" I asked. "The missing girl could have decided to ditch her life and throw in with the vamps."

"We won't rule her out, but it doesn't make sense that she'd meet her accomplice on school grounds. Why argue, and why now, when it's been days since she disappeared?"

Okay, he had me there.

"So what next?" Bobby asked.

"Well, from the conversation Gina overheard, I'd say our most likely bet is that someone is lacing the school food or maybe water supply with something hinky. Clearly, the aggression isn't supposed to be part of the package, but we don't know what it *is* supposed to do. Anyway, that makes Belladonna look like a top suspect, since she'd have access through the food service. Gina, you're part of her gang. I want you to learn what you can. Maya will back you up. Bobby, on Monday I want you to be the last in your period on the cafeteria line. Charm the lunch ladies. You've got the power. See if they've seen or suspected anything or if any of them seem suspicious themselves. Their records are clean, but you never know. Rick, you're going to the school clinic on Monday. Fake a blinding headache or something that'll get you painkillers. Bring them back for analysis. It's a long shot, but with Hailee's mom having a pharmaceutical connection, we should check it out. Also, I want water samples from the school fountains."

"But—" I piped up, shooting a glance at Rick. I could take him down if he took what I was about to say the wrong way, but I'd probably spill Sid's coffee all over his computer doing it. With my luck, it would probably come out of my paycheck. "Rick's behavior changed without him ever going to the clinic—when he attacked me at the hospital."

Rick gave me a nasty grin from across the table. "What makes you think I need a chemical excuse for that?"

"Settle down," Maya ordered. "Gina's got a point."

"Yeah, and it's on the top of her head," Rick muttered.

"Of course," I continued, provoked into opening my mouth again, "there could be some *other* drug going around school that's accounting for your behavior. Steroids?" I'd heard about 'roid rage, but could it happen so fast? No way he'd been able to get any during spy school.

He struck the table hard with the flat of his palm. "I'm not on steroids."

We all stared at him.

After a minute, he took a visible breath to calm himself. "But I have been buying the school lunch."

That seemed to clinch it. The comment I'd overheard the girl make, about some people "bringing their own," made total sense if they were talking about school lunches ... or, yeah, maybe painkillers or bottled water, but that seemed a whole lot less likely.

"Have you tested his blood?" I asked, looking between Sid and Maya, who exchanged a glance themselves.

"Yeah," Sid admitted. "Some organic compounds— wolfsbane and the like. No commercial drugs. More like spell components. We're already trying to trace who's bought these compounds in bulk over the past few months. Whatever's going on around here is not natural, but we knew that already. The trace is slow going. Most of these ingredients aren't dangerous on their own, so there's no regulation, no one has to sign for them. And if they pay cash ... "

The table shook as Rick's fists both crashed down at once and he stood, bumping the table yet again, rattling his coke and Sid's coffee. "You took my blood?" he railed. "When? When I was sleeping? Is that why you have me on this case? The token human, like the canary in the coal mine. Cage me in and read my entrails if I kick off?"

He seethed and for a second seemed almost larger than normal, like rage had puffed him up too big for his shell to contain, like violence was going to burst out of him at any second.

Sid stood as well, slowly, hands held loosely at his sides, which I recognized from training as being the way to keep your options open, ready for action. "Calm down, Rick. You cut yourself shaving yesterday. We tested the blood you blotted. As for the entrails, you knew this job was dangerous when you took it."

"And anyway," I said as calmly as I could, "if you die, you come back as one of us, right?"

He took a deep breath and, just that quickly, the scary went out of him. "Right," he admitted with a wry grin that made him look all boyish, not at all the Mr. Hyde he'd been just seconds ago. "I forgot. Guess I . . . got carried away."

He sat back down and for a moment no one knew what to say. "Maybe you'd better bag your lunch for the next few days," I said, still calm. I was hoping that as his vampire dam, should he ever turn, maybe I carried some kind of clout.

"Yeah," he answered. "Maybe. And we should probably organize some kind of boycott at the school … just in case."

"Great idea," Maya said, jumping on the chance to get things back on track. "Gina, you said you have a vegan friend?"

"Lily," I offered.

"Think you could stage a protest?"

I grinned. "Food fight, protest, boycott. I'm your girl."

"Good. And while you're at it, get the goods on Bella."

"Done."

"Now, for Hailee."

"I'll do it," Bobby jumped in. I scowled at him and he added, oh-so-helpfully, "She, ah, seemed to like me when she showed us around. Shouldn't be too tough for me to interview her."

"Good," Maya said, proving she had no grasp at all on the meaning of the word. "Does anyone know Marissa?"

"You got a picture?" Rick asked.

I thought he was just being a horndog. Sid eyed him dubiously, but typed a few strokes onto the computer and swiveled the screen around to face us. On it was a slender brunette with big doe eyes in an otherwise unremarkable face.

"Sure, I know her," Rick said. "She's always taking pictures. At practice. In the halls. I can think of an excuse to talk to her."

Maya didn't say "good" this time, probably just as worried about Rick as I was.

"Okay, we're settled then, I guess. Gina, do you have any plans—"

My cell phone interrupted us and I smirked. I knew Ulric would find the number eventually. I might even be extra nice to him, since Bobby had volunteered to cuddle up to Hailee.

But it was Lily on the other end. "We're going to the mall," she said without preamble. "You in?"

"Mall," I mouthed to the others.

Sid waved me to continue.

"I don't know," I answered, putting on the world weariness I'd felt this morning. "I'm not even up yet."

"Well, the guys are—all but Gavin, anyway—and I've already had to talk them out of a raid on the hospital. We need to distract them with virtual reality games. Bella and I are going to need reinforcements."

"A raid? Why?"

"The hospital's got us blacklisted. Bram's parents' orders. We can't get in to see him. No one will tell us anything because of the damned HIPA laws. It's criminal. The boys are going to take out their aggression on Zombie Death Squad...and Bella needs a new pair of fishnets."

"What happened to her old ones?" I asked.

"There's a hole."

I wasn't even going to *think* about the logic of that.

"I can be ready by noon," I said.

"Good. We'll pick you up as soon as Gavin gets his raggedy ass out of bed."

We hung up and I looked at the others. "Gotta go. The mall beckons."

"Not until noon," Maya said. "We all heard you. First mug shots, then mall."

I sighed and settled back in my seat. "Okay, set 'em up. I'll knock 'em down."

Sid opened up a file and turned one of the laptops toward me. Head in one hand and my other hand on the touch pad, I scrolled through screen after screen of mostly artist drawings of vamps. A few had actual photos that must have been taken before their deaths. There were notations below the photos but they had to be in code, because I sure couldn't understand them and there was nary a vowel in the bunch. None of the vamps looked like the guy who'd attacked Hailee in the woods. I still shuddered just thinking of his eyes. And none looked like the surfer boy from the school.

I was ready to give up when I found him. Not the surfer boy, but the other. Shark eyes…feral, depthless, and inhumanly dark.

Sid noticed when I stopped scrolling. "You find something?"

He and Maya both came over to look. Maya gasped. It was as much emotion as she'd ever shown.

"It can't be," she said. "It's not possible."

"What isn't?" I asked. I clicked on the photo and up popped a full dossier. I glanced at the name—Grigori Yefimovich Novykh—but it didn't mean a thing to me. "It's *your* database. I didn't make him up."

"The man has more lives than a cat."

Bobby and Rick were now behind me as well, everyone looming over me to stare at the screen.

"No way," Bobby said in hushed reverence. "The Mad Monk!"

I turned my head as far as I could to look at them. "What? Who is it? For God's sake, someone spit it out."

"You'd know him as Rasputin," Maya answered, her eyes never leaving the screen.

"No freakin' way!" I said. "You mean that accent was real?"

"Or it may just be someone who looks eerily similar," Maya said, almost hopefully. "I mean, the last reported sighting of Rasputin was over a decade ago in Afghanistan. The field agent reported him dead."

"But with his powers of hypnosis..." Sid began.

Maya's phone blipped an alert and Sid stopped. Maya tore her gaze away from the screen to check her phone. She paled and turned the volume up for us to hear. Her phone was tuned in to the news and had alerted to an item of interest.

They'd found the missing kids. Dead of exsanguination.

Suddenly it was far less exciting that history had come to life, that our very first mission pitted us up against the larger-than-life figure who'd advised doomed Romanov royalty until they were all put to death in the Russian Revolution.

A bloody end... just like Tyler and Teresa's. Speaking of which, tonight was the third night since Red Rock. If Tyler and Teresa had been dead since their disappearance, and if blood was exchanged rather than merely taken ... well, tonight was the night they would rise again.

11

I would never let on how freaked I was at the idea that I'd come face-to-face with the Mad Monk. I figured a trip to the mall might be just the thing to drive it out of my mind. Meanwhile, the boys had to stay behind to plan a raid on the morgue in case Tyler and Teresa had joined team vamp, even though *I* was the one with the absolute perfect wardrobe for B&E. Where else did you wear basic black if not break-ins and funerals? The morgue was a two-fer.

But Maya and Sid couldn't just spirit Tyler and Teresa's

bloodless bodies away like they'd swept the whole thing in Ohio under the rug. Everyone had been looking for the missing kids and, thanks to the news, everyone knew they'd been found. If they rose... well, we'd have to see what we could do to cover up the bodies' vanishing act. But I couldn't figure out why, if they *had* been turned, Raspy and his cabal had let the bodies be discovered. Sloppiness? Sheer insanity? Some kind of trap? Maybe they didn't call Raspy "The Mad Monk" for nothing.

I asked these question, but Maya assured me they'd covered all their bases. Sid would play lookout during the raid and knock out any surveillance equipment, since although it wouldn't record Bobby, it would catch Rick or mysteriously opening and closing doors. Maya was to be my back-up at the mall.

•   •   •

Bella made space on the bench seat next to her when the hearse eventually pulled up at my door and I slid into the back. Byron was driving, and, wonder of wonders, Ulric was sitting in the passenger seat rather than trying to play footsie with me. That left me facing Lily and Gavin, who still had bed wrinkles on his neck and cheek. There was a funny feel to the mood, like they'd all just stopped talking about me when I popped my head in.

"What's up?" I asked, as the door closed behind me and Byron peeled away.

They all exchanged glances, as if deciding who was

going to be the sacrifice. Lily finally threw her hands in the air like she was disgusted with the rest of them.

"Something you want to tell us?" Lily asked, looking me pointedly in the eye.

I was baffled. Had Lily known I wasn't really at home when she'd called, that I'd been lying about just having woken up? Had someone seen Maya drop me off back at my apartment? She'd left me two blocks away and I'd walked, so no one should have spotted us together. But the more I learned about magic's actual existence, the more I understood that "should" was more of a guideline than a rule, kinda like not wearing white after Labor Day. Anyway, something was up. You could cut the tension with a knife.

"Like what?" I asked cautiously.

"Superpowers, kicking butt, what you're really doing here."

"*What?*" I was starting to sound like a broken record.

"Come on, Gen, Ulric *saw* you last night."

I looked at him, but he was gazing stubbornly out the front window. I couldn't tell if he was mad at me—though I couldn't figure out why he would be so suddenly—or mad at them for pushing me.

"And lots of people saw you at Red Rock," Lily continued. "We were all kind of blitzed, but it's obvious something's up and we want to know *what*."

"There's nothing going on," I swore.

Bella gave me a *look*, her dark eyes full of disbelief.

"Hey, great performance last night, by the way," I added.

The ghost of a smile twitched her lips, but she said, "Are you trying to distract us?"

"Yeah. *See*, I suck at that kind of thing. And in case you haven't noticed, subtlety and secrets are kind of lost on me. If there was something going on, trust me, you'd know it."

"Reeally?" Bella asked, drawing out every sound.

"Cross my heart and hope to die." What the hell, I already had a head start.

Ulric turned finally. "I told you guys she'd tell us when she's ready. You can't expect her to give up her secret identity just like that."

I growled. "*What secret identity?*"

"Come on," Bella said. "*Geneva Belfry?* No one has a name like that."

Ah ha, I had an answer for this one. "Oh, that's right, *Belladonna, Ulric*, rag on my name. For your information, I changed it when I got emancipated from my parents, when I wanted to disappear. What's your excuse?" I looked at each one in challenge, but it was totally lost on Byron and Ulric in the front seats. "Geez, I thought I'd left all this crap behind."

I crossed my arms over my chest and looked away from them all. My gaze hardened with a hurt I hadn't really expected to feel. It shouldn't have mattered how they felt about me. I'd earned it, and anyway, this was *a job*. But somehow it did matter. If I let down my guard just a little, I might even squeak out a blood-red tear. Wouldn't *that* give them something to talk about?

"I'm sorry," Lily said quietly. "We didn't know."

I nodded shortly, still fighting the emotion, feeling just a little badly for using it against them, especially Lily, who seemed genuinely to care, but at least the pressure was off. How the whole emancipation thing explained my super-powers, I didn't know, but I'd learned as an only child with no one else to blame that the best defense is a good offense.

Bella reached over and silently gave my hand a squeeze where it crossed my arm. "Parents suck."

Ah, common ground.

•   •   •

By the time we reached the mall, everything seemed forgot-ten—or at least no one was willing to bring up the subject again. Lily was determined to make things up to me with a wheat-grass smoothie, which sounded about as appealing as ice-cold blood. I pled allergy, but I don't think she was convinced.

Byron, Ulric, and Gavin carried their conversation into the mall, debating the merits of Zombie Death Squad over Bone Crusher IV (and whether IV was really an improve-ment over III), and I surprised myself with a huge sigh of relief. I didn't know why I'd gotten so choked up. Sure, they'd welcomed me as one of their own, no questions asked, like the family I'd had to leave behind in Ohio, but—I couldn't afford to care again. This was an assignment. When I fin-ished, I'd be gone. A new mission, a new identity, everyone left behind, just like my old life. My parents. My hometown. All my BFFs. Best if I hardened my heart now.

"Hey, you okay?" Bella asked, nudging me with her elbow. I'd barely even noticed that we'd wandered into a small store with the absurdly cutesy name of *Salem Stitchcraft*. I'd been so lost in my thoughts I'd forgotten to browse.

"Yeah, fine." I forced a smile and tried to see her as a suspect. It would make everything so much easier.

She didn't comment on the obvious lie, instead holding up a pair of stockings with a web-and-spider design all over them. "What do you think of these?"

"Hot," I answered with a smile.

I picked an off-black pair of stockings with a classy backseam from a wall hanger, and grabbed a tiny black-and-purple pleated skirt that ought to make my legs look a mile high.

"What about this?" I asked the girls.

"Ulric's eyes will fall right out of his head," Lily commented.

"Oh good. I can add them to my collection."

They both laughed. It felt good—or bittersweet, anyway. I'd missed this. It had never occurred to me that goths might be people too … in the shopping, mall-crawl, gal-pal kind of way. Dammit.

Lily picked out a bustier-style top that fastened around the back of the neck. The fabric was, I had to admit, pretty cool—a red skull-and-crown pattern with some metallic thread running through for sheen.

"Come on, let's go try things on."

We headed for the fitting rooms.

Lily came out of her stall holding the halter up behind her neck and spotted me avoiding the store's full-length mirror. I couldn't see what I looked like, which nearly killed me, but given the widening of her eyes, Bobby would plotz when he saw me. To complete my look, I'd have to replace those platform Mary Janes I left behind at Red Rock.

"Can you help me with this?" she asked.

I scooted quickly past the mirror and pushed her hair aside to get at the clasp, but there wasn't nearly as much of it as there should have been. She'd brushed it over carefully, but now that I was close, I could see how uneven it was in one section, like a hank of hair had been ripped out. I touched Lily's head, forgetting about the halter and almost letting the straps slide, exposing her to the world.

"Gen!" she called out.

I regained control of the straps just in time.

"What happened here?" I asked.

She hissed out a breath. "Hailee." The name sounded like a curse the way she said it.

Bella came out of her dressing room, sporting the webbed stockings beneath a pair of black shorts with a black top with slashes running through it, exposing a cool blue cami.

"If you haven't had a run-in with her yet, you will soon," Bella said, picking up on the conversation as she stepped between us to peer into the mirror. "She thinks she's all that and a bag of chips. Wants to give the world a bimbo Barbie makeover."

"And she started with Lily's hair?" I asked, wide-eyed.

"We kind of got into it," Lily said briefly. "A little help here?"

I dropped her hair and moved on to fastening the neck clasps for her.

"Did you report her?" I asked.

Lily and Bella exchanged a knowing look. "What's the point? Her mom's pals with the vice principal. Hailee can do no wrong. Anyway, I gave as good as I got."

"When was this?" I asked.

"I don't know, a week or two ago. Before you got here. Why?"

I had to think fast. "I'm thinking about revenge ... you know, best served cold and all that."

But really, it was because I wanted to see whether Hailee had been a witch—spelled b-i-t-c-h—*before* the weirdness started or only after, which would tell me if she was more likely to be a participant in the problem or a victim of the general insanity. With someone like Hailee, it was often just too tough to tell. And now that I knew Lily had been attacked, like Bella, only different, I had to add her to the list of suspects. After all, she'd been there the night I overheard someone conspiring with Grunge Vamp, and she hadn't been with me at the time. On the other hand, neither had Bella or Hailee or Marissa. I couldn't rule any of them out.

"Speak of the devil," Lily said, looking straight past us to the store entrance, where the very blond bimbette we'd been discussing stood with her posse. Her throat, where

Raspy had bitten her, was hidden beneath a Coach scarf. Beige... how appropriate. She'd rifled through one of the racks posted outside the store to draw in customers and had come up with the most hideous dress she could find—a pumpkin-orange monstrosity with black tulle underneath. She held it up against herself and made some kind of comment that sent her flock into a fit of laughter, like she'd actually made a decent joke. Wait, was three a flock, a posse, or a pride? Certainly it wasn't enough for an entourage.

I wanted to yell something about orange really being her color, picking up the carroty tones in her hair, but for once I used a little restraint. I wasn't there to right the social wrongs of the world, and anyway, I might have to pump her for information at some point, as unappealing as that sounded. Furthermore, Maya was supposed to be my back-up. I hadn't seen her, but I knew she was around somewhere. She was probably just being subtle and sneaky and all those other S words (like spy and surveillance and spook). I wanted to show her that I could behave. Didn't mean I had to like it.

Lily didn't have any such concerns. "Hail, that dress is *so* you!" she called across the store. "Right down to the extra padding."

Hailee's face turned redder than the dress in hand. Her narrowed eyes searched Lily out like a sniper scope. Her glare was almost enough to cut us down where we stood. "Are you suggesting I stuff?" she snarled.

"You saying you don't?" Lily asked, pouring on the disbelief and cocking a hand on one hip.

Hailee hissed and launched herself into the store. The sales girl who'd been restocking shoes and watching us out of the corner of her eye flew to intercept, but she didn't have to worry. Hailee's buds, who had more sense than she did, grabbed her, clucking like a bunch of hens in a way that was probably meant to sooth.

"Watch your back," Hailee spat out as her friends led her away. "Some day I'll catch you alone."

"Thanks for the warning," Lily called. "You'd just better hope I never catch *you* without your posse to back you up."

That settled it—posse, then.

Hailee tried to launch herself toward us again, but she was held fast and dragged away.

"That was fun," Lily said, looking positively perky. "What do you say we celebrate with a smoothie?"

"What *is* it with you and smoothies?" Bella asked. "Do you have any idea how much sugar they have?"

"Enough to ride a natural high," Lily answered back. "Then we can tear the guys away from killing zombies and make them take us to a movie. *The Taxidermist XII* started on Friday."

"Oh, please, number eleven was so lame," Bella complained.

"Yeah, but this one's got Milan Jokavic in it."

"That hot guy from *Wicked Dead III*?"

I smiled, letting it all wash over me, feeling for the first time in far too long like a normal teen. Friends, enemies, shopping...

Suddenly the sales girl was standing in front of us. "You want me to ring those up?" she asked, clearly anxious to be rid of us. We all exchanged looks.

"What the hell," Bella said. "I'll wear mine out."

Still, she disappeared into the dressing room to gather her stuff, as did we all, though I took an extra few seconds to change because I didn't have the right footwear for my outfit … yet. I met up with them at the counter.

When it was my turn, I passed over my governmentally supplied credit card. I hadn't thought to ask how it worked. Did they cover my expenses or would the bill be taken out of my paycheck? Whatever. Backseamed stockings were classics, and the sight of Bobby's tongue dragging on the floor would be more than enough to justify the skirt.

"Shoes before smoothies?" I asked, as the sales girl handed me my bag.

"Sure," Bella said, surprising me because it always seemed that Lily was the decision-maker of the group. "I know just the place."

•   •   •

We didn't actually get back to the guys for another hour, and it was *another* after that before the next showing of *The Taxidermist XII*, which is how I learned that even goths liked Dance, Dance Revolution. Unfortunately for Lily and Bella, I was at minimum semi-pro. We'd even started to gather a crowd by the time we had to leave for the film.

We girls sat on one end of the row with the guys toward the center, arguing all through the opening credits about how Gavin's target gun on the last game had been—or not been—misaligned, cheating him of the high score he deserved. When the hushing started he subsided into a pout.

A third of the way through the movie, the *Mission Impossible* theme started playing in my head like a ring tone. Bobby and Rick must have begun their infiltration of the morgue and somehow, Bobby's mental mood music was bleeding through to me…

And then suddenly it cut off. There was complete and absolute silence except for the screaming onscreen. The hero and the too-stupid-to-live heroine were still alive for the moment. I was struggling to care, struggling not to panic over what might be happening to Bobby, when something very pointy poked the back of my neck and my skin tried to crawl away from it.

Wood, I knew instantly. A stake. Whoever was behind me knew exactly what I was and didn't seem any too happy about it. I could imagine that I'd made some enemies— the jocks, the pretty-girl posse, *Rasputin* and his minions, though I still couldn't believe it was him. I mean, even *I'd* paid attention to that part of history class. But only a few people knew we were going to see this particular movie at this particular time and I was sitting with them. Someone had sold me out.

12

The stake piercing my spine was starting to draw blood, and I was temporarily thankful to the goth god that black was good for disguising blood stains. Too bad my mesh probably wasn't machine washable.

"Do you *mind*?" I asked, half turning in my seat.

"*Move*," the woman behind me hissed.

I sighed dramatically, then cringed since it ground the stake closer to my spinal column.

Bella glanced over at the disturbance, and I took it as a

cue to excuse myself before she got wise to what was going on and put herself into harm's way. Of course, if Bella was my Judas it wouldn't matter, but I didn't know and couldn't risk her.

"Smoothies go right through me," I explained as I slipped past Bella into the aisle.

She nodded, twitched her legs aside, and turned straight back to the man being mangled onscreen.

Once I was clear, pointy-stick woman grabbed me by the waistband of my jeans in a grip way too intimate for not having bought me dinner first. I hissed, and she poked me again. This woman was *so* going down, especially if the back of my neck scabbed over and kept me out of pigtails for the foreseeable future. Not that I was really into pigtails, but a girl liked to keep her options open.

I pretended to stumble, to rip myself from her grasp and escape the stake, but the Prickly Princess only tightened her grip on my jeans until it was a damned good thing I didn't have to breathe.

We were all the way to the exit doors, me mentally calling out to Bobby, hoping he wasn't in trouble himself and that he'd get Maya a message wherever she might be— which was supposed to be *right freakin' here* covering my butt. I ran through my mental catalogue of moves—elbow jab to the solar plexus, stomp on her insole, stop, drop, and roll—but the stake was a wee bit intimidating.

As if she could read my mind, the Prickly Princess moved the point to right between my shoulder blades. I was no science geek, but I was pretty sure that from there it was a straight shot to my heart, assuming no pesky vertebrae got in the way.

"Don't even think about it," she hissed in my ear.

"About what?" I asked, a little too loudly now that we were away from my friends, at least some of whom were probably innocent. "My mind's a blank." I was hoping to make a commotion, but all we got was a round of "Shhh"s and a crew of prepubescents in the back glancing between us and the screen to see which might become more interesting.

"Move," she said again, emphasizing her point in a very literal way.

I moved, pulling open the heavy theater door and stepping out into the hallway. I had barely registered Maya in my peripheral vision when she struck—grabbing me by the shirt and ripping me from the Prickly Princess' grip. She spun me toward the doors that lead out of the theater entirely.

"Go!" she yelled, tossing me a set of keys. Prickly snarled and charged Maya, but was blown back by a snap kick to the face. "Go for the car! Pull it around."

She didn't have to tell me twice.

I bolted for the outer door that led to the parking lot, hoping I'd find the car up front and center, because the lot was jam packed. I cruised the rows, pressing the *unlock* button every few steps and waiting for the car to beep back at me. I hoped Maya was still winning.

I found the car, planted myself behind the wheel, and laid rubber to the theater entrance, only running over one traffic cone and nearly leaving the undercarriage behind.

Maya was in the breezeway between the inner and outer doors, holding a slumped Prickly, Pummelled Princess under the arms like some drunken scarecrow. She seemed a strange choice for a kidnapper or assassin—light brown hair under a silk bandana, big round sunglasses that made her eyes look owlish, a camel-colored sweater, a darker brown full-length skirt and matching boots, and big gold hoops in her ears. She looked like an escapee from a 1970s Nick at Night rerun.

"Sid missed a check-in," Maya told me as I jumped out of the still-running car to help pour PP into the trunk. My heart contracted, nearly kick-starting again in panic. Sid was supposed to be Bobby's back-up...and Rick's. If he'd been put out of commission...

I slammed the trunk down hard over the unconscious Prickly Princess. If she was connected with Bobby's disappearance...if he'd been hurt in any way...she was dead meat. The kind that didn't rise again.

"I'll drive," Maya said, leaping into the driver's seat before I could protest. I slammed into the shotgun seat, and she took off before my door was even shut.

"I heard Bobby in my head for a bit," I told her, holding onto the dash for dear life, my matte black nail polish nearly cracking from the strain. "He just cut off. You don't think—"

"I don't speculate," she said, proving the stick was still firmly lodged up her butt. "We'll find out soon enough. We're headed to the morgue now. If we don't find them there, Rhoda here can tell us where they are."

"Rhoda?" I asked.

"Old television reference. Never mind, you're way too young."

She drove like a bat outta thrift-store hell. It was dark, even darker than it should be at six thirty in the evening, which meant that clouds had moved in while we'd been at the Galleria. No sooner had I thought it than big, fat raindrops started to fall, playing on the roof like *Taps*. I squashed that thought faster than a cockroach with last year's clogs ... not that I'd be caught dead in a pair of clogs. Anyway, no *Taps* because Bobby *wasn't* dead. I'd know. We had a psychic connection. One that didn't seem to be operational right now, but still ...

Bobby, Bobby, please Bobby, I burbled in my head. *Come in, Bobby.* If he were anywhere within range of my psychic cell signal, he should answer. Unless ... unless it couldn't go through lead or whatever, like Superman's vision. I didn't want to think of him in a lead-lined box. I knew what that meant.

"Can't you drive any faster?" I asked Maya, even though she was already about to blow the land-speed record.

"Not without hydroplaning."

"That's like water surfing right? No traction, no resistance, more speed?" Which only went to show that I was totally not thinking clearly, because it was a night like this one that had ended my first life. Of course, we'd had help then—a little side-swiping and a spin-out into eternity. What didn't kill you made you stronger, right?

Maya didn't dignify that with an answer. We were less

than a block away from the back entrance of the ME's office, the one leading toward the morgue, when we spotted Sid's car and what looked like his body, slumped down in the driver's seat with his head resting against the window. I heard Maya suck in a breath with a "*Dios mia.*" It was the first time I'd ever heard her curse. I thought it was a curse, anyway. Beyond *nachos*, *huevos rancheros*, and *mariachi*, my Spanish was pretty nonexistent.

She launched herself out into the pounding rain and circled the front of Sid's sedan to yank his door open and catch his body as it fell out. I grabbed the plastic laminated road atlas out of her back seat and held it over my head as I followed.

"He's breathing," she said when I crowded her, trying to get my head in out of the rain.

Sid flinched like he was having one of those falling dreams and had just suddenly woken up.

"What—?" He stared at us, and his pupils were huge. "How did you get here?"

"Sid," Maya said urgently, "where are the boys?"

"Boys?" He stiffened up then and his eyes fastened on her with laser focus. "Crap! The boys! I was out?"

"Like a trout," she answered.

He drew his hand down over his face, now wet from the cold spray bouncing off us from the open door. "It was a setup—the vamps let those bodies be discovered. They must have been waiting for us."

"Which means this isn't just some rinky-dink operation,

some teen witch messing with the ley lines and unrelated vamp activity."

"So they've got the boys?" Sid asked, apparently slow coming out of his funk.

"It looks that way, but we've got an ace in the hole." Maya looked back at her trunk.

"You go question your catch," he said. "I'll search the scene here and let you know if I turn up any leads on what's happened or where they've gone."

She didn't look all that anxious to abandon him. "You've got cell signal?"

Sid checked. "Three bars."

"Good. Keep it close. Check in every half hour."

"Will do."

We were drenched when we got back to the car, all except for the very top of my head which had been covered by the road atlas. The rain had blown in sideways and dripped off the atlas until water wasn't the only thing pouring down. Black dye ran from my never-been-washed T-shirt, covering my arms like blood. I was a vision.

The trunk thumped and the car bucked. Maya cursed.

"Keep it down back there!" she yelled, like the junk in the trunk would pay her any attention.

It seemed like the longest ride of my life. Wet and uncomfortable, calling out to Bobby with no answer coming back. Just waiting until I could get my hands on the Prickly Princess. I was looking forward to trying out my interrogation techniques.

13

I was out of the car before Maya had even shut it down. The automatic garage door was already descending, shutting out whatever we were about to do from the eyes of the world, as if anyone was out to see or care in the pounding rain. It gave me the sense of intense isolation, which was good, because I couldn't be trusted with our hostage—not when her people had Bobby. My conscience twinged, but it was as obsolete as dial-up Internet. I'd gone vamp. For all I knew, I didn't even have a soul to worry over any more.

But I *did* have Bobby, and *nothing* was going to get to him on my watch.

I had to wait for Maya to pop the trunk, which she did via her car key remote thingy, so she was far enough away not to take a boot to the head. And to level a gun at the trunk as it opened. I'd never even seen the gun on her, and I wondered if it was loaded with special bullets or if she was counting on the regular kind to slow the Prickly Princess down for recapture.

Prickly Princess struggled to sit up and then looked around wildly for a way to escape. Just in case Maya's human reflexes weren't fast enough on the trigger, I grabbed the trunk lid before it was fully open and clocked PP on the head, part precaution and part payback for Bobby. I was careful not to hit hard enough to knock her out. After all, we still needed answers.

"What did you do with Bobby?" I asked her, my voice so harsh I hardly recognized it as mine.

Her eyes grew hard as radioactive rocks. "They said you'd be the easy one."

"They lied," I answered. "Where. Is. Bobby?"

Maya stood beside me, adding the weight of her stare and the barrel of her gun.

Prickly's bandana had come askew in the trunk and she glared back at us through lost strands of hair, her gaze hot enough to sear, making me think of the Su Surus song "Long Gone Dead":

Your eyes are like a knife
Stabbing daggers, end my life

But I won't come home to you
Best believe I have a clue.

It was totally off the topic of torture and interrogation, but sometimes my mind had a soundtrack all its own.

"I could grab a sun lamp and some holy water," I said to Maya.

"These are wooden bullets filled with birdshot," she answered. "Either one would hurt like the dickens." Okay, I got it. She was bad cop.

Prickly Princess blanched and went ballistic. Zero to sixty is no time flat, trying to launch herself out of the trunk at us, but she was hardly in any position for grace and it slowed her. Maya shot her in the shoulder before she could get anywhere, the silencer making it sound more like an air gun than a deadly weapon. If the Prickly Princess hadn't fallen back into the trunk, whimpering in pain...

My phone chose that second to ring, a ridiculously perky song under the circumstances. I reached for it, hoping against hope that it was Bobby but thinking it was probably Sid, even though I had no idea why he'd call me and not Maya.

"Hello."

"Hey, it's Lily." I was so surprised it took me a sec to process.

"Lily, what's up?" I tried to sound casual, but I eyed PP as I said it to see if she'd react to the name. No such luck.

"Where are you?" she asked. "The movie ended, like,

twenty minutes ago and you never came back from the bathroom."

It was exactly how I'd expect her to sound if she thought I'd ditched her and the others. I quickly ran through possible excuses.

"Sorry, it's my parents … one of them sicced a PI on me, who was kind of insistent that we talk. She caught up with me at the theater, and I didn't want to make a scene, so I bailed."

"Bailed where?"

Okay, now I was suspicious. "Why?" I asked, eyes narrowing, even though she couldn't see them over the phone.

"Because we're at your place and you're not here."

"My place?" I asked, voice raised to near screech. Maya winced.

"We were worried about you."

"Well, don't be. I needed some alone time."

"Sounds like you need a restraining order. Or a party. Lucky for you, we've already got one started."

"What?" My voice rose again. Pretty soon I'd shatter glass.

"When you weren't here, we kind of just let ourselves in."

I wondered if steam was coming out of my ears.

"Well, let yourselves out."

"See, that's the thing—we met up with a bunch of others outside the movie, and we were all pumped up. When I couldn't reach you, we swung by and Trey Banyon had a few six packs … "

"What?" I almost roared. I so didn't have time for this. Bobby was in trouble. All I wanted to do was bleed info out of the Prickly Princess and hunt Bobby down. Save the day. I looked at Maya, who had an eyebrow cocked questioningly at me. "Wild party at my place. Could be a trick to lure me out by myself."

Maya thought about it a second while Prickly wailed into the silence. Maya twitched the gun menacingly. "I'd like to hear myself think," she rumbled. "Unless you have something meaningful to say." PP shut up.

Note to self: Never get on Maya's bad side. P.S. Find out if she has any other side. Maybe send pound cake.

"You've got to go," Maya said after a beat. "The mixture in the blood is too important to risk. If the wrong people rummage in your fridge and get their hands on it..." *Oh crap.* Bad vamps immune to sunlight. So not good for our team.

"Okay," I answered reluctantly. "I'm out. But you call me the second you have anything."

Look at me and my bad self, making demands on the lady with the gun.

"I promise," Maya said.

I nodded and dashed for the door to the house, not willing to open the garage and expose our doings to the world. Behind me I heard Maya say, "Go ahead, make my day." I hoped she was talking to the Prickly Princess. I ran through the house to the front door and hit the stairs just as Sid was pulling into the driveway. Perfect timing, since it had only just occurred to me that I didn't have any wheels.

"I need your car," I called to him. Every sopping second I stood outside was one more our enemies had with Bobby, and potentially with the blood.

He rolled down the passenger-side window. "What?"

"I need wheels!" I wasn't going to explain the rest standing out in the open. Luckily, he didn't make me.

I heard the locks pop as he said, "Get in."

For once, I didn't hesitate to obey orders. "My place and step on it," I said, like he was some New York cabby.

He took off. "You going to tell me what's going on?"

"Kids," I said, "at my place. All alone with the blood supply."

He gave it more gas. If we weren't careful, we'd have a police escort, which, considering that it would close down the party, probably wouldn't be the worst that could happen.

"You find anything at the morgue?" I asked while he drove.

"We've got two more vamps now. Tyler and Teresa busted their way out of their body vaults. Wonder what the coroner will make of that."

"Focus here. *Rick. Bobby.* What about the important stuff?"

"Gone. They put up a fight, that's clear enough, but there wasn't much blood. No sign of where they were taken. No calling card or matchbook like in the movies. Nothing."

Bobby? I called out again mentally. *Come in, Bobby. I lo—miss you.* I'd almost said the "l" word, that's how upset I was. Even though I knew it gave guys way too much power. Even though I knew he had to say it first (my mama had raised me right). But, darn it, I did, and if he was too stupid to realize it by now, well, then he was too stupid to live.

I didn't mean that! I said immediately to the universe at large. *If you bring him back to me, I'll give up mall crawls for a month ... except, you know, as my spy gig demands.*

The universe, like Bobby, wasn't answering.

• • •

Visibility was nil, which made Sid's speed a dangerous thing. A couple of fishtails slowed him down to a semi-sane speed, but it only transferred the insanity to me. I needed to shut down the party and get back to the interrogation, stat.

Cars lined both sides of the street in front of my apartment, and I knew it wasn't going to be that easy. I had Sid let me off around the corner so no one would see me with him, and slogged my way back to the apartment. Within four steps I was a drowned rat in danger of being washed away down the sewer grates. Every gust of wind slapped me in the face with another lash of icy rain. My goose bumps could qualify for their own zip code.

Music blared from my building, which was at least still standing. I couldn't be certain it came from my place. Buildings that smelled like feet didn't attract the best-behaved batch of tenants. If doors weren't slamming and running feet overhead didn't sound like they were coming right through the ceiling, it probably meant the neighbors were partying out that night. I imagined so anyway. I hadn't actually met many of my neighbors. Probably a good thing when it came to the guy in 3B, who liked to cook with garlic and onions. Just sniffing the air one floor above was like inhaling mustard gas. Luckily, for me breathing was optional.

I wanted to go in with guns blazing, not that Maya had trusted me with one. I wanted Bobby's mystic mojo so I could compel everybody out. But I didn't have either of those things, and since the party could well be a trap to flush me out after the failed kidnapping, I needed to be on my guard.

The adrenaline pumping through my veins apparently stimulated my brain cells too, because by the time I slammed open the door to my apartment, I had a plan. More or less.

The first person I saw was Ulric, whose mouth fell open at the sight of me: dye-stained arms, rain-matted hair and all.

"*Don't,*" I warned him, in case he was about to speak. In the mood I was in, it would get his head permanently ripped from his body, and I didn't have time for the rigmarole of a murder investigation.

I stomp-squished off to my room, leaving a river of rain behind me. People cleared a path as I went, either from my glare or in reaction to my sogginess.

My room was crowded—a girl and guy necking on my bed, and the rest ignoring them and talking amongst themselves.

"OUT!" I yelled, loud enough to rattle the hangers in my closet.

Everyone but the couple on the bed took one look at me and decided not to argue. I rung my hair out over the cozy couple, knowing I'd be sleeping in a wet spot later, but gratified by their yelps and instant separation.

"OUT!" I repeated, pointing at the door so there could be no mistake. "Now!"

I slammed the door and locked it after them, then stomp-squished toward my closet. I pushed open the accordion doors and two kids nearly fell out—one of them Gavin. The other Lily.

I didn't know who was more shocked—Lily or me, but her face turned the color of strawberry sorbet. She must have seen something of my rough night in my face, because she wordlessly grabbed Gavin's hand and led him to the door without me saying another word. She fumbled with the lock, but finally they were gone and I was alone.

I stripped, dropping my wet clothes right there on the awful carpeting, grabbed a shirt from a hanger to towel myself off with, and dressed as quickly as I could in dry clothes. I felt dangerous. Warmer and drier, but no less homicidal. Was it adrenaline overload, or that same buzzy feeling I'd gotten on Red Rock when the ley lines got jiggy with me? It didn't matter.

I stomped back out—not that anyone could hear me over the awful sounds coming out of my boom box. Someone must have brought some CDs, because none of mine sounded like people torturing cats and running nails down blackboards. I wanted to find the offending thing and turn it off. Or smash it to pieces. I wasn't picky. Either way would probably clear the place out eventually. But I couldn't let anyone leave before I made sure they wouldn't be taking my bottled blood with them. While I was at it, I'd see what, if anything, I could learn.

If it were up to me I would have been halfway to the kitchen, but Lily and Gavin headed me off in the hallway.

"What happened to you?" Lily asked. Her face was pinched with concern. Either it was real or she belonged on stage next to Bella.

"Who did it?" I asked, glaring from her to Gavin, hoping I'd be able to tell if either was guilty just from the looks on their faces.

Both were convincingly baffled. "Did what?" Gavin asked.

"Ratted me out to my folks. I changed my name. Moved to a new town. They found me. Dad did, anyway. Someone had to have finked. I won't blame you. He's sneaky. He's even got a 'Have you seen this girl?' MySpace page with some sob story about me being a runaway," I improvised. "Reward and everything. People have fallen for it before. And there's no way his people found me at the mall by accident."

Lily's eyes were as big as saucers and Gavin's lit with a weird manic light.

"There's a million ways to find someone these days," he said, "and only so many ways to hide. Did you know—"

Lily slapped him. "She doesn't want a lecture right now. Do you, Gen? What can we do? You're not skipping town, are you?" she asked, seeming genuinely upset at the thought.

"Not this time. Whoever's behind this is going to have a real fight on their hands."

She looked confused, and I realized my words didn't sync with my cover story, but they'd been straight from the heart. Whoever orchestrated things didn't know who they were dealing with. I was the *easy* one, the Prickly Princess had said? Total fighting words.

"Where's Bella?" I asked.

Lily blinked. "Bella? You don't think she—"

"Where. Is. She?" I repeated.

My teeth were starting to sprout, and the careful enunciation wasn't even about menace. I hadn't eaten in hours; the overdose of earlier action and adrenaline was starting to make me punchy. And Gavin's little love bites had brought the blood rushing to the fore of Lily's lily-white neck. Hickeys were nothing more than burst blood vessels. And all that blood, spilling uselessly ... I swallowed, shocked to be thinking of my friend as an all-you-can-eat buffet.

"Geneva?" Gavin said, a strange note in his voice. "You okay?"

I snapped out of it then, and looked at him and tried to focus. I could actually see the pulse point of his neck ... pulsing.

"Bella?" I asked again.

"Last I saw her, she was in the kitchen," Lily said. "But that was, like, a half hour ago."

Good enough. The apartment wasn't that big. I would

find her. If she was in the jam-packed living room, I couldn't see her. She wasn't in the kitchen either, which only left the bathroom—and I surely wasn't following her in there. But before I moved on, I checked the fridge. My bottled blood had been pushed way to the back of the shelves to make room for beer and wine coolers. I breathed a huge sigh of relief and grabbed a beer for appearances' sake. I twisted off the cap, threw it on the counter with a couple dozen others, and went in search of Bella. Maybe I could find the weak link before I shut the party down, and the trip wouldn't be a total loss.

There was a teeny, tiny landing off the kitchen that a real estate agent might call a balcony... if she was really desperate to sell. I figured I might as well try looking there before squeezing myself back toward the living room, contorting around guys I didn't even recognize who were sloshing beer onto my carpet and using the close quarters as an excuse to cop a feel. The mood I was in, they might just lose a limb... or something they'd *really* miss.

I gave the back door a solid push, since someone at some point had brilliantly painted the door and jamb together so that they stuck shut. It slammed open, striking against the railing mere inches away and stopping, too tight in its frame to even bounce back. One glance told me I had the place to myself. I turned to head back in, only to be blocked by Ulric. He stepped out behind me, close enough to nearly knock me off the balcony so that he could clear enough space to shut the door behind him.

He didn't know what he was doing. My hunger surged

at the thought of the two of us alone on a dark slab of concrete the size of a welcome mat. No witnesses. No moon that could be seen. No light but the little spilling out through the kitchen window.

"Lily says you're on the warpath," he began, oblivious to the fact that he looked good enough to eat.

I took a step closer. He didn't move back, but his face took on a look of bafflement. Ulric liked the chase. He seemed to like the control, putting me off my game. I wondered what he'd make of me as the aggressor. *What about Bobby?* a little voice in my head asked. *That's about l—uh… lust,* I told it. *This is blood.* But I wasn't sure. At that moment, I wanted to bite into Ulric's neck like I'd never wanted anything in my life. Not Bobby. Not my favorite pair of stilettos or my slinkiest dress.

I breathed him in, starting at that musky place right in the center of a man's chest and raising myself up on my toes to continue along his collarbone to his neck.

"Geneva?" he asked. His voice barely worked, but that was okay. I didn't want him for his mind or his mouth.

"Shhh," I said softly, brushing my lips over his neck. I could feel his pulse beating beneath, taste the faint tang of sweat filming his skin.

He put his hands on my shoulders and pushed me away, just enough so he could get a good look at me. He swallowed.

"Gen."

I pushed him back against the wall, hard enough that he "oooph"ed when he hit. It was like I was two people—the one in charge, who was going to bite him no matter what the other me had to say, and the other, trying to tell me that this was not what I came for. Inside the apartment was my stash of blood. I could make it. But the blood would be cold and there'd be witnesses. *Here* there was Ulric. Warm and willing—or at least he would be once I bit him and the vamp venom or whatever took effect.

"Gen?" he said again, maybe just a trace of panic edging his voice.

A last little bit of sanity made me give him a chance. A small one. "Say yes," I ordered, not certain I could control myself if he said "no."

"Yes," he breathed, like he couldn't help himself either.

I rose onto my toes, grabbing his shoulders for support, and nuzzled his neck once to brush away any stray strands of hair before opening wide and sinking my fangs deeply into his neck. I sucked, and the world exploded inside me. Sensation was a flash flood. Overwhelming. Incredible. Heat and power. Energy and adrenaline. Life. Liquid life. A roaring, racing fountain of youth.

One of us moaned, but I had no idea where I started and he ended. It was so good. So ... I was no longer on my tiptoes, and that's when I realized Ulric had been sinking, weakened by the blood loss. The realization shocked me enough that my fangs retracted, sliding out of his throat as I went from holding his shoulders to holding him *by* the shoulders as he slumped into me. I eased him to the concrete floor, since I didn't have so much as a folding chair in the little space.

"Wow," he said, his butt bumping the floor.

I looked at him, seeing him perfectly in the dark as his head rolled from its resting place against the wall to lock eyes with me—those deep, dark eyes filled with something akin to worship.

"Was't good for you?" he asked, a sleepy slur to his voice. Guilt hit me in the gut. Me. Guilt. It was the one thing I didn't wear well. Usually, I returned it with the price tag still attached, but today I smacked right up against a serious no-returns policy.

"Great," I muttered truthfully. Then, louder, "You stay right there. I'll get you something to drink."

I tried to tell myself I was no worse than a blood drive, buying him off with cookies and juice.

I turned to head back in, to scour the apartment for anything edible that might have been brought in, and came face-to-face in the doorway with Bella and her ice blue eyes, such a cold contrast to Bobby's warm blue.

"Geneva, Lily said you were looking for me?" she began, in that fey voice of hers.

If she noticed Ulric slumped down on the balcony, she gave no sign, but I don't know how she could miss him.

"Bella! Thank goodness. Ulric collapsed. Low blood sugar or something. You stay with him while I grab him something to eat."

Bella didn't budge, and suddenly I *knew.* I'd suspected, but I hadn't realized how much I'd been hoping I was wrong, and how little I'd committed to the idea that I was right—until now. It hurt. I mean, we'd gone *shoe shopping* together, for God's sake. It didn't get more bonding than that. But apparently it meant nothing to her.

She saw the moment I came to my conclusion, and the mild look fell from her face like a mask. "You're not going anywhere," she growled, lunging at me. I leapt aside, but got tangled up in Ulric's sprawled legs and didn't get as far away as I wanted—far enough away to avoid the hypodermic needle Bella had been hiding behind her back. She sank it deep into the muscle between my shoulder and my neck and pushed the plunger. My whole body caught fire, burning me up from the inside out. "Garlic juice," she said in my ear.

I couldn't answer. I couldn't do anything but fall to the cold concrete floor of the balcony, clawing at myself as if I could rip open a vent for the fire within to escape.

Then she did something, but I couldn't tell what, couldn't see through my parboiling eyeballs. Whatever she did jostled me one way, then the other. And suddenly she was treating me like a life-sized marionette, jacking me upright with the aid of a rope wrapped around the railing. Soon I was standing, or some semblance of it, eye-to-eye with Bella, who hesitated for a moment on the verge of doing whatever she was about to do. "I'm sorry I have to do this," she said softly. "It's the only way in. As soon as I hit my weight goal, they'll preserve me in time. Young, skinny... eternal."

And then she pushed me over the rail. I had a moment of terror as I plummeted, forgetting in my fear that I would live through the fall.

I braced for impact, but something caught me before I

hit the ground. Arms. Thin, almost skeletal. Wrong some-how, as if there was an extra joint, and then a voice in my head, as different from Bobby's as hightops to heels.

Ah, pretty, pretty, pretty. At last you're mine.

Alistaire...the psycho-psychic, subtly twisted beyond recognition by some magic gone wrong. The one who'd called me *chaos*, back in Ohio, and nearly eaten my BFF while inexplicably not eating me. He'd left the clear under-standing that it was a one-time deal.

I hoped the garlic would kill me, because if not, Alistaire surely would. And Alistaire liked to play with his food.

14

Alistaire licked my nose like a pit bull puppy. In fact, he resembled one—his eyes sharp and predatory, watching me like a chew toy he couldn't wait to sink his teeth into. And those teeth ... too many of them, all razor sharp. He'd been a man once, then a vampire, and now something other, though I still didn't know exactly what. He still wore a man's shape ... except when he didn't.

"Ah," he said, closing his eyes to savor my taste. "Such a unique vintage, but there's something ... different about it. Word is that you and your boy have become daywalkers. The stuff of legend."

Above us, Bella gasped, calling Alistaire's attention to the balcony. I guessed he wasn't who she'd been expecting, so I took a quick look around for her conspirator—he or she might distract Alistaire enough for me to bolt, assuming my body would cooperate. This hope was quickly dashed. Grunge Vamp lay on the ground just feet away, his throat torn out.

"Don't worry, morsel," Alistaire said, his voice that eerily high-pitched singsong I'd hoped never to hear again. Like a possessed Tiny Tim. "Your friend will heal and return with a message to his sire... *my* sire, in fact. Grigori and I go way back, to the beginning. And what's a little blood-letting among friends?"

Bella's eyes were wide, white showing all around them like a spooked polo pony. She looked ready to bolt. "Hold!" Alistaire commanded. She clutched at her head, and I knew he was pushing his thoughts on her. I remembered the feeling—it was like an entire swarm of hornets in a stinging frenzy, swelling your brain until it would burst your skull wide open. Alistaire's mind was not a pretty place. Nor particularly sane. "You tend to your friend and leave me to mine. Forget everything else. Everything you've seen and heard."

She collapsed to her knees, to where we could no longer see her head above the balcony rail. I hoped he hadn't pushed too hard. Even with what she'd done, I couldn't quite want her dead. Not that way. On the other hand, once her compatriots knew she'd failed, what I wanted might be a moot point.

"Alone at last," Alistaire said then, as if Bella were already forgotten. I was used to having a man's total attention, but not this way. Alistaire looked at me as though he'd like to crawl around in my skin while I was still wearing it. "I've missed you. Oh, so much. I promised I'd be back. But where is the boy? Have you lost him?"

The hornets swarmed in my head as he forced his way into my thoughts. He couldn't control me. None of them could. It was my single claim to fame beyond the whole eternal-life/sharpened-senses thing. But he could rifle through my mind, reading my thoughts. There was no finesse to it, and the disaster he left in his wake was like the devastation of a smash-and-grab rather than the precision of a cat burglar. I had to fight him.

I tried. For Bobby. But the heinous hornets burned their way through the walls I tried to throw in the psycho-psychic's path. I had no control over my body because of Bella's injection, no control of my mind. I sagged to the ground, weeping precious blood at the pain.

"Ah hah," Alistaire said at last, still holding me so that I couldn't slide away entirely. "So he *is* here. I heard of the council's plan to turn humans into the sheep they are, and I knew who they would call. Who else but the ancient alchemist, the Mad Monk?"

The glee was such that he could have been crowing about winning the lottery or a lifetime supply of hair gel. It was stupid to feel hurt that *I* wasn't his ultimate prey. But then, I'd already been caught, hadn't I? And so easily. By a scrawny little goth girl I should have known better than to trust.

Alistaire shook me out of my thoughts by lifting me up, throwing me over his shoulder, and sprinting off. Around my building he went, across the street between all the cars, past another apartment building so similar to mine they could have been twins, and finally into the woods beyond. He kept on going at full speed, regardless of the branches that whipped like canes and the downed logs he vaulted like a pro. At least my face was sheltered, but my nose bumped against his bony back with each step, and I took some satisfaction in the idea that I was bruising it as well... but not much.

"Slow down!" I called, but it came out more like, "Oh ow!" and he ignored me entirely.

Then his steps changed, and we seemed to be bounding up a set of stairs. *In the middle of the woods?* I wondered, but I couldn't see. I could only hear the sound of a door splintering as he punched into it to get around the lock. Then we were through. It was a few more seconds before he threw me down on a couch that smelled of decades worth of dust and dirt.

Suddenly, I could see again—vaguely. The garlic still coursed through my system, leaving me weak and wonky, but it didn't matter—there wasn't much to look at. We were in a dark room with wood-slat walls, a few blurry chairs, and a makeup counter running the length of one wall topped with what looked like the general contraband of a theater company. Costumes lay discarded over the back of the musty couch and, now that I squinted, I saw something that looked like, and I sincerely hoped was, faux flesh sitting on the counter among the makeup sponges and containers.

I shuddered, hot and cold at the same time as though I had food poisoning. I hadn't sweated since I'd gone vamp—just one more side effect—and if my sweat was anything like my tears, I couldn't be doing wonders for the couch.

Alistaire, studying me, said, "It is perfect, no?" He laughed, and it felt like spiders with pin-prickly legs climbing over my flesh. "Humans use this as a haunted house. In less than a month, this place will be crawling with people, so kind as to cater to each other's fears. Delicious."

He squatted in front of me and I shrank back as much as I could. His black, pointed tongue came out to lick my nose again. "Yes, delicious. Except for the garlic aftertaste. But that too will pass. And then, pretty, pretty, you will be mine."

Oh joy. Oh rapture. I had to escape before then. As soon as I could think, see, and walk properly.

Alistaire ran his hands over me until I wanted to puke, but stopped when he came to my cell phone. He pulled it out, wiped the screen where my makeup had probably left a smudge, and dialed. I was baffled. First, over the idea that he had any friends to call.

"You have this number now," he said into the phone. "Call me when you're ready to make a deal ... *Pater*."

Okay, cold, I was definitely running cold. Frozen with shock, actually. Was it the Mad Monk he was calling? Of course, it all tied together, the Mad Monk was his sire ... but a vampire *pater* or a human one?

Either way made a stunning kind of sense when I thought about it. Both Raspy and Alistaire had cheated death several times over the course of their lives, Alistaire most recently when his vampire daughter, Bobby's dam, had tried to take over Alistaire's territory by killing him off but only managed to twist him into the fine figure of a boogeyman he was today. Maybe it ran in the family. If I remembered rightly, when Rasputin wasn't advising Russian royalty or messing with magic, he was partying the night away, which usually ended with a partner or two, unless rumors of his affairs were greatly exaggerated. He probably had more offspring than I could shake a stake at. Had they all ... been vamped? The very idea was terrifying, way more terrifying than anything ever developed for this haunted house we were in.

Alistaire slammed my phone shut and tossed it onto the counter beside the faux flesh. It made a gruesome still-life. "Don't move," he ordered, before leaving the room. Only for a minute, sadly. Not long enough for me to get my muscles to respond and escape. He came back with a roll of duct tape that he used with wild abandon, taping my legs to each other and binding my arms against my sides like some low-end seaweed wrap.

My blood-sweat made the sticky side of the tape gummy almost instantly. I vowed that when I got free, I was going to use up the rest of Alistaire's nine lives in the most painful way possible.

It was either close to dawn or the garlic poisoning was truly catching up to me. I struggled to keep my eyes open, to find the strength and means to escape, but exhaustion hit me like a two-ton truck, and I slept like the dead.

15

I didn't wake up so much as come to with a jolt. All around me was darkness. That didn't mean anything, necessarily. Alistaire had put me in an inner room, but I had a strong suspicion that I'd sweated away the suncreen potion along with the garlic and a good bit of my blood. Lord only knew what had been happening while I was out. At least the other vamps would have been out as well... unless someone had bitten Bobby and gotten enough of *his* bonus blood into their system. Or... and this was the part I really didn't want to think about…what if they'd drawn vials of his blood or taken something to study, maybe even learned what went into our enhanced bottles of blood so that they could recreate the special mixture for themselves? I was pretty sure that letting the baddies *and* state secrets slip through our hands qualified as total mission failure. What if the Feds decided to cut their losses, and us along with them?

I had to get free, find and rescue Bobby, destroy any of his blood Raspy might have managed to draw, and stop whatever plans they had involving my schoolmates and their bizarre behavior.

I struggled against my duct tape bonds, all gummy with the sweat and uck. I thought that if I shimmied just right I ought to be able to get the tape worked up my body and onto my neck and shoulders, freeing my arms to lift it the rest of the way. Alistaire had to be close by, but he must have slept in another room. Maybe I reeked that much. The *garlic*, not me really, although between the lovely blood sweat, the gummy glue, and last night's run-in with the rain, I had to be a vision of fugliness. I wondered if I'd have time for a miracle makeover before rescuing Bobby.

But first, someone had to rescue *me*. As if in answer to my plea, my cell phone rang out some song I didn't know the Feds had considered sufficiently gothic to preprogram. Then Alistaire entered, with that weird triple-jointed grace he had, and lifted the phone from beside the clumps of faux flesh on the counter. I wondered if he'd even know how to answer it, since he didn't seem to carry one of his own, but he didn't have any problem at all.

"Hello."

I strained my super-vamp senses, which were back, thank goth, now that the garlic had sweated out of my system, stinging my skin but no longer poisoning me from within. Hey, a rhyme. I wondered if Byron would be able to use it in his death poetry. But I was getting distracted.

"Alistaire, what has it been?" I could hear the voice on the other end of the line asking. "A century? More. And yet when we come together again, you steal from me. It is a very poor welcome." It was that heavily accented voice I now knew to be Russian rather than Transylvanian. Big diff.

"I left Dimitri alive," Alistaire answered. "A token of good will. But you have something I want. You know how I deal with things that stand in my way."

Alistaire actually sounded coherent. No *pretty, pretty* or *morsel* in his speech. If it hadn't been for the veiled threats, I'd have been convinced he was a pod person.

"As you are standing in mine."

"You've made it clear enough that I have always been inconvenient," Alistaire snapped.

Oooh, Alistaire had daddy issues. It all seemed so... so... Dr. Phil. Jerry Springer. Whatever. There was some majorly rotten fruit on that family tree. I wondered if it was intel I could use.

The man on the other end of the phone—Raspy— sighed. "I'm too busy for your games. What is it you want?"

Alistaire was silent, making him wait for an answer, taking some of that time Raspy didn't have. It was a total power trip.

"I won't give you the formula," Raspy said quietly, as if Alistaire had asked.

I was no brain surgeon, but even I knew saying that was stupid. It told Alistaire exactly what Raspy most wanted to protect and gave his enemy the upper hand. Then I realized something else . . . Alistaire made his own *pater* nervous. His own infamous, I-can-hardly-believe-he's-not-deader dad was babbling like a late prom date.

"I want the boy," Alistaire said, which made my heart clench. He couldn't get his hands on Bobby. I wouldn't allow it.

"Impossible," Raspy answered. "The council has already sent someone to collect him and bring my reward. If *you* bring the girl to *me*, I will cut you in on it. I know you don't want to deal with the council yourself."

Ah, so sonny boy wasn't the only one who could make veiled threats.

"You've never had any idea what I want. It's not your formula, *Pater*, or the money. I've never cared for your petty games with the mewling monkeys. I hunt higher on the food chain."

Raspy was silent at that, and I wondered what was going through his head. Schemes, no doubt. But then he said, too quickly, "Very well. You can have the boy with my blessing, though I can't speak for the council. In return, you will leave town immediately. Without first interfering in any of my plans. You will not visit the high school or harass any of my minions on the way out of town. I will know if you lie."

Wow, you'd have thought he was a lawyer, closing up

all those loopholes. I held breath I didn't need, waiting to see what Alistaire would say.

"Once I have the boy, I have no reason to stay. Or interfere," Alistaire answered. "But in return, *you* will not stop *us* from leaving. You will not act against us in any way."

"This time," Raspy agreed. "When next we meet—"

"To the death," Alistaire said.

"Da. *Yours*. I will send instructions."

With no good-bye that I could hear, he was gone. There was silence for a good second or two. I debated leaving it that way, but in the end, it was just too much for me to keep my mouth shut.

"You don't *trust* him, do you? Besides his word—and, *hello*, bad guy here—what's to stop him from setting up an ambush and taking me away instead of giving up Bobby?"

Sure, at least Bobby and I would be together again, but it kinda seemed like a frying pan/fire situation. I didn't imagine we'd live long enough to enjoy it.

Alistaire cocked his head, birdlike, to look at me as if I were a worm he'd seen out of the corner of his eye, who he didn't want to startle before he swooped in for the kill.

"There is nothing to stop him. And no, morsel, I am not so foolish as to trust. You will have to decide whose side you will fight on. Mine? I am after you and your boy only. I will have to free you to help me. You will both have your powers and your chance of escape. I have no interest in enslaving your friends, controlling those over whom I am already master. *Pater*… Father," he said, with an inhuman twist of his lips, "has ever wanted to play shepherd and lead the sheep to the slaughter."

"How do you know I won't run?" I asked stupidly.

"How do you know I won't look forward to the chase?" He licked his lips. "So, morsel, will you deal with the devil? Will you sacrifice yourself for the sheep?"

He was a madman. Not that I hadn't known it before, but to ask me to fight at his side for the privilege of remaining his prey...insane. On top of that, you totally didn't ask a fashionista about sacrifice. When I'd lived and breathed, every time I walked by a Starbucks without turning in, every time I ordered my mochachino with two pumps not three, no whip, and fat free milk, I was making a sacrifice. Every time my parents cut up my credit cards for going over the limit...I *knew* pain and sacrifice.

Besides, my choice was none at all. Say "no" and stay behind, or say "yes" and chance saving the day: rescuing Bobby, stopping the plot that put my peeps in danger. Ulric, Lily, Gavin, Byron, and Bram...they'd gotten under my skin. And even if they hadn't, the villainous vamps weren't likely to stop there. Today Wappingers Falls, tomorrow the world. Easier to stop them sooner rather than later—simple logic and laziness, really. Which meant that for now, the enemy of my enemy was my friend.

The promised instructions came after five agonizing minutes, during which Alistaire didn't bother to ask about my decision. Being psychic and all, he probably already knew. I hated that. Whatever vision he'd seen must have worked out in his favor or he wouldn't have been so smug.

But I was chaos. He'd said so himself not so long ago. I just had to find a way to bust destiny's groove.

"An abandoned warehouse," Alistaire said, staring at the text message on my cell. "How ... inventive."

"You can't seriously be planning to show. He's got minions. You've got ... me."

"Don't underestimate yourself, my dear," Alistaire answered. I wondered if that meant I'd been upgraded from "morsel." "He will be expecting a captive, not a consort."

"Oh, I am *so* not your consort."

He only smiled in that chilling, psycho-killer way of his.

"I'll drop you off before we get there and go in alone. You'll follow and surprise anyone who closes in behind me. Try to stay on the periphery if you can, and get your boy out of it if opportunity strikes. If you are within Rasputin's range, your powers won't work. He'll be able to control you."

"Is *that* what's going on with Bobby's powers? Rasputin somehow cancels him out?"

I suddenly wondered if my resistance was more of a genetic thing than a special *me* thing, like my green eyes and fashion sense. If Alistaire was planning to face down Raspy, he had to be counting on some resistance of his own. But if our resistance *was* inherited, it had skipped Bobby and all his vampire siblings. Okay then, maybe I was still special. Whew, crisis averted.

"Rasputin is a power vampire. Even before he came to the blood, it was power that sustained him. Energy."

Like in the ley lines, I thought. If he was feeding from

them, it was no wonder the Feds had noticed fluctuations. Dips as he fed, spikes as the energy renewed itself afterward.

"Don't worry, he's all yours," I promised.

"Do you drive?" Alistaire asked.

"Do you?"

"How do you think I got here?"

"Grew wings and flew," I answered flippantly.

Alistaire looked at me as though he could look *inside*. "Is that what you'd do?"

I blinked. Was that even possible? "Let's say yes. How would I go about that, again?"

The psycho-psychic laughed, and I imagined dogs the neighborhood over trying to bury their heads in their paws to tune him out. "I jest," he finally said. "Even the great Rasputin can no more than levitate." *Good to know.* "Of course, *he* cannot walk in the daylight as you can…yet."

Yeah, we totally had to get Bobby away from him. Then away from Alistaire. Then…okay, one thing at a time.

"My car is out back," he said.

His car, as it turned out, had been someone else's first, someone who was, in fact, still in possession of it…in a sense anyway. I heard a faint moaning as we approached the car. Alistaire escorted me by the arm, partly to keep control of me and partly, I thought, to keep me upright after all the blood I'd lost with the garlic. The moaning sound stopped when we got close.

I looked at Alistaire, who smiled, revealing more than the normal vampiric number of pointy teeth. "A little something for the road," he said. "Please, help yourself."

Sloppy seconds. My lips peeled back in distaste even as my eye-teeth grew in anticipation. "I couldn't."

"You mistake this for a suggestion. I need you in top shape. You *will* feed, or I will slit his wrists and feed him to you. *That* is your only choice."

He opened the door for me and thrust me in. My gaze caught on the body in the back seat, nearly hidden under a dark blanket except for the face, which was turned toward me, eyes wide and staring, as if the man was in shock. That might very well have been the case. I couldn't really take the moral high ground about feeding from the vein after I'd gone all fangtastic on Ulric, but if Alistaire had already been feeding, I wasn't sure how much more this guy had to give.

Alistaire enjoyed my dilemma—I could tell by the smirk on his face as he got behind the wheel. Driving looked way weird on him, just like my cell phone had. "Eat," he ordered.

I considered the greater good—saving Bobby, stopping the Mad Monk from mind-messing with my friends, finding the strength to fight Alistaire himself when the time came. I wanted to think it was that which drove me to it, not the low tones of the man's heartbeat, pumping all that glorious blood. I'm almost sure it was the greater good.

Before he could flinch, before he could soil himself with fearful anticipation, I swiveled in my seat, reached back over the center console, and grabbed him by the blanket, scrabbling for the right hold to bring him to me. His eyes barely widened before I bit down on his neck and sweet, hot life flowed into my mouth. I gulped it down as quickly as it flooded in, lost in the sensation until the flood began to ease, and I realized the heartbeat within the folds of the blanket had gone thready. Barely there.

In horror, I tore myself away from the man—the nameless man I'd nearly killed, and might yet if that heartbeat didn't steady.

Alistaire laughed. "Saving me the leftovers, morsel? Think that alone will slake my thirst?"

I didn't answer, concentrating instead on listening for the heartbeat all the way to the warehouse, ignoring the stolen strength that rushed through me.

"It should be another two blocks ahead, on the left," Alistaire said, the good cheer gone and his high voice making him sound like a ventriloquist's dummy on speed. Dummies had always freaked me out.

He'd no sooner finished speaking than he reached over, grabbed the door release on my side with one hand, and pushed me out with the other. The car swerved, and I went flying into a ditch on the side of the road, cursing him the whole way. I guessed I was supposed to look like somebody he'd disposed of, like the man I'd drained nearly to death.

Oh, the psycho-psychic was going down … hard.

My jeans were totally shredded up the side in a way that some people paid big bucks for, but then, so was the skin beneath, in a way people paid plastic surgeons bigger bucks to fix. Luckily, my vampitude would take care of it, if I lived that long. I pulled myself to sitting so I could survey the area, playing up the pain and injury for all I was worth in case there were any witnesses. It was an Oscar-winning performance, but if anyone was watching they didn't bother to applaud, let alone throw flowers.

I changed tactics, keeping as low to the ditch as possible and creeping forward, doing the crocodile crawl I'd learned in basic training. If I was lucky, I'd continue on unseen, not attract any baddies or even a good Samaritan who might call attention by trying to help me out. I hoped that if anyone did see my movement they'd think I was a stray dog or cat or something.

I knew I'd reached the warehouse when the grass all around me got so tall I no longer had to worry about being seen. "Abandoned" meant no one to care for the property, which suited me just fine.

If ever there was a time for those lessons on stealth mode from super spy training to take, it was now. I peered through the tall grass and weeds as best I could and saw a white cement-block building with the words *Freight Liquidators* stenciled on the side in peeling blue paint.

If Raspy had set guards, they were on the inside—which made sense if you didn't want anyone to notice sudden activity at an abandoned site. I took a deep breath, just because it seemed the thing to do, and started through the high grass, aiming for the front door because, well, it was closest. If it didn't open, I'd try around the side.

Apparently, fate had decided it'd had enough fun at my expense, and no one stopped my mad dash to the door, which was, miraculously, unlocked. And then fate blew me a big fat raspberry. The door creaked as it opened, alerting the two goons inside. They flew at me from the left and right. One male, one female. Nice to know ole Raspy was an equal opportunity destroyer. I had a split second to recognize Tyler and Teresa, the resurrected teens, before they were on me.

I ducked them as they came—sometimes petite actually had its advantages—but they didn't oblige with any cartoon head-bashing. Instead, they each locked onto one of my arms. In probably my best move from training, I kicked one leg back as far as it would go for the momentum, then swung it fast-forward, flipping myself up and over between the two like they were nothing but an uneven parallel bar. Oh sure, it wrenched my shoulders out of their sockets, but the goons—or anyway, our missing students-turned-vamps—lost their handle on me. Before they could regain it, I bolted down the hallway, past pasteboard partitions that mimicked offices and into a vast echoey room directly ahead—the main part of the warehouse. There were doors that shut it off from the "office" area, and I slammed them shut with my shoulders, popping each one back into place as I did. It was only then, as the terrible teens slammed up against the door behind me, that I realized the lock that secured the doors had been busted and there was nothing but me and my size-four self between them and total access.

I spun, lightning fast, to put my back against the door so I could brace myself with my legs ... and came face-to-face with vampdom's best and blightest: Raspy, Grunge Vamp—*Dimitri*, Alistaire had called him—and the psycho-psychic himself. Bobby was in the midst of them, bound in rope. It looked like each side might grab an end and use him as the center knot in a twisted tug of war.

"Gina!" he shouted.

"Bobby!"

"I thought we were going for *stealth*," Alistaire hissed.

"The door squeaked." I shrugged. "Anyway, you know how I like to make an entrance."

"Gina?" Bobby said again, his brows lowering in confusion over those killer blue eyes.

"Later."

I didn't want to be short with him, but something about all this felt very, very wrong. Alistaire had been expecting a trap, which only made sense, but why hadn't Raspy already sprung it?

Unless—

My gaze flew straight to his, those shark eyes, empty of emotion but filled instead with an unholy light. They flickered off to the right, and I whirled in time to dodge a dart coming at me. I deflected another one headed for the psycho-psychic with the blade of my hand, like I was some kind of ninja warrior princess. It was all instinct, like knowing which fashions would be hot and which not.

But, of course, it left the doors I'd been body-blocking undefended, and Raspy's minions burst in behind me. As much as it creeped me out to do, I went back to bony back with Alistaire in the middle of the warehouse floor while Raspy and his flunkies converged.

The someone-in-the-shadows to the right tried the darts

again, and this time Alistaire, prepared, saw his coming. He caught it in midair and, lightning fast, sent it toward Raspy, who deflected it with a snarl and launched himself at Alistaire in revenge. It had to be what the psycho wanted, because he met Raspy with a savage glee in his eyes. At least with the two in a clinch the shadowy shooter probably wouldn't risk a shot with the dart gun.

But I didn't have time to worry about them. I rushed for Bobby. Before I could get to him, the teen vamps I'd blown past on my way in grabbed me from behind, one going for a handful of hair as well as my arm so I couldn't try the flip trick again. I shrieked and tried to yank myself loose, willing to risk a bad hair day or two, but I couldn't pull far enough away with them holding my arms.

Bobby yelled for me, and Grunge Vamp yelled for Rasputin, some kind of warning. I whipped my head around to see what was going on in time to witness Raspy crumpling to the warehouse floor, a dart lodged in his shoulder. The shooter had missed Alistaire.

Dimitri rushed to him, and Alistaire turned as if to fight, but Dimitri was more interested in catching his fallen prophet than taking his place in the battle.

"What have you done?" he yelled into the shadows.

Rick stepped forward. *Rick.* It took a second for me to process it. Whose side was he on? Had he missed Alistaire with that dart intentionally or accidentally? According to Rick, who was trying to fast-talk his way out of trouble, it was accidental.

Not that Dimitri was listening. He was too busy speaking Russian at Rasputin, whose shark eyes struggled to remain open, to focus their hatred on Alistaire.

"Kill him," he ordered Dimitri, forcing the breath out.

Grunge nodded, one brisk bob of the head. He lowered Raspy softly to the ground and leapt over his prone form to go for Alistaire. But the psycho-psychic had better reach, and clasped a claw to Dimitri's throat before Dimitri could lay a hand on him. Alistaire used the momentum of Dimitri's charge to swing him toward me and my two captors. Dimitri's body hit mine dead-on, knocking me back, ass over anklets. Raspy's welcoming committee lost their grip on me. I rolled with the blow, and popped up ready to run.

I looked at Alistaire, afraid I was getting away only over his dead body and wondering how I'd succeed where so many had failed. But Alistaire had grabbed hold of Raspy and unfurled those oddly jointed legs to the point where he managed to look like a giant jumping spider.

"Later for you, morsel. I promise we'll have our time together. I have your scent." The thought sent fiery-footed millipedes up and down my back.

Then he was off, carrying Raspy over his shoulder much as he'd taken me the night before.

My ninja princess reflexes kicked in again as Rick and the terrible teens all tried to tackle me. I dodged them, zigzagging toward Bobby to grab him on my way out, again wondering if Rick had missed on purpose or if our side was just that good. Target obtained, Bobby and I darted for the warehouse's back doors.

"Can you open them?" I asked Bobby as he struggled to keep his feet under him, his arms too bound up for balance.

"I think so. Something gave when ... Rasputin went down. *Rasputin*. I still can't believe it!"

"Escape now, marvel later," I ordered.

Bobby slowed as he concentrated, and the other vamps were almost on us when I heard the sound of something metal sheering off. Then Bobby kicked the loading dock doors open and we were off into the night, the baddies breathing down our necks.

It was another second before Bobby's ropes unraveled and fell to the ground, the better to trip up those on our tails. We put on an added burst of speed and hit the road in advance of them.

"Can you call Sid and Maya?" I asked. The psycho-psychic still had my phone, and I sure as heck wasn't going to find and fight him for it.

We dashed into the street, putting cars between us and our pursuers as I felt Bobby send out a burst of power, like an all-points bulletin. Super spy training had really ramped up his abilities, and I was sure wherever our handlers were, they'd hear his telepathic call. We just had to keep ourselves free for pick-up or back-up. If we could keep the goons busy until the Feds arrived, maybe we could round up all the rotters. All but the biggest baddies anyway, who, if we were lucky, were off taking care of each other.

The hench-hord gave up on us as we dodged the traffic,

freezing at the edge of the road as if cutting their losses on us to concentrate on going after their kidnapped kingpin. Or maybe what scared them off was the ten-ton truck bearing down on them...or my ninja warrior moves. Anyway, when I looked over my shoulder again, they were turning back toward the warehouse. I eased up on my full-out run to look for some street sign or mile-marker we could call in.

16

Bobby and I were in the back seat of Sid and Maya's spy mobile, chugging blood like it was the best stuff on earth. The warehouse was deserted by the time back-up had arrived, so there was nothing left to do but debrief and regroup. Between gulps of body-temperature blood, I filled the Feds in on everything that had happened. Bobby interrupted when I got to the part about Rick.

"I'm not so sure he's gone over to the dark side. Not really. When Rasputin got the jump on us at the morgue, my powers failed. Rasputin was able to control us," he added with a blush. "Not like I can; not both of us at once. Just one at a time. I heard the vamps talking, and that's what the experiment at the school is all about—lowering the will and raising the suggestibility of the kids so that it doesn't take any power at all for mass mesmerism. If it works, the vamps will find a way to slip their formula to entire human populations. We'll—they'll—become meals on wheels. The council contingent that's coming in, the one Rasputin planned to turn Gina and me over to, they aren't coming here just for us. Rasputin's perfected the formula. The trick was to make it in gaseous rather than liquid form. They're going to unleash it tomorrow night."

"Where?" Maya asked.

"I don't know. That's why I didn't suggest we grab Rick on the way out. He's on the inside now. They still need human student minions, at least until their plans all come together. I figure if he can get word to us, he will. He may have helped us already. I'm not so sure he hit Rasputin with that dart by accident."

I'd wondered the same thing, but somehow when Bobby said it, I wasn't so sure. Wouldn't it have made sense for Rick to let us in on things somehow? Or had it all happened too fast?

"But there's nothing going on at the school tomorrow night," Sid protested.

Wait a minute—it couldn't be that easy, could it? The reason Raspy needed human minions … the way to put together a spontaneous gathering of guinea pigs … "Word's going out!" I cried.

They all looked at me like I'd lost my mind. "Come again?" Bobby asked, giving me the benefit of the doubt.

"The parties. That's how they happen—word goes out: meet up here at such and such a time, BYOB."

"It makes sense," Maya admitted. "But how will we know where and when?"

"For one, if the formula's now in gaseous form, they won't want to release it into the open air. It'd be too spread out. Too uncontrolled. So, if we're right, and it's a party they're planning to arrange, it won't be anywhere like Red Rock. It'll be somewhere enclosed, indoors … *like a warehouse*," I said.

But Sid was already shaking his head. "They won't use that place again, now that we know it's there."

"Well then, it's your job to search out all the likely abandoned or vamp-owned places in the area that are big enough for a rave."

"And if it's a private home?" Maya asked.

"I'm sure you've got the home addresses of all the major players so far."

"But will they still try out the new formula tomorrow?" Maya asked. "Since Rasputin's missing in action?"

"The better question is whether Raspy's recruits can afford to fail with the eyes of the council on them. I think they'll have to rally."

"If this is all going down tomorrow night, we don't have a whole lot of time," Sid said. "It's going to be a late night and an early morning. You two are going to school tomorrow. See if you can get yourselves invited to a party."

"Meanwhile," Maya said, "I'll get a strike team out to that haunted house in case Alistaire took Rasputin there. I'll put them on stand-by for tomorrow night."

Cool! I'd like to be able to just order out a strike team … or a personal shopper, for that matter. I wondered how long it would take to work my way up to management.

When we got back to base, we all had jobs to do. Bobby's was to try to mind-speak to Rick. Mine was to find out what Bella had told the other goths about my sudden disappearance and her hand in it, so that I was sure I *could* show my face around town. Maya and Sid had the oh-so-exciting job of researching possible party places. Maybe I didn't want to be management after all. The field had so much more to offer.

I borrowed a disposable cell phone, one of many that Maya happened to have on hand, and dialed Lily. She had that, too—Lily's digits—which was a good thing because I'd never had a head for numbers.

It rang until I was sure it was going to voicemail before a voice came on and said, "Y'ello."

It *might* be Lily, if she'd first gargled razor blades, then washed them down with whisky.

"Lily?"

"Who's this?"

"It's Geneva."

I heard scrambling and fabric sliding over limbs. "Geneva! Are you okay? Bella said you fell off the balcony.

Ulric said you'd been pushed, but he wasn't making a whole lot of sense. Then we couldn't find you." She fell silent, waiting, I guess, for me to fill in the blanks. "I have to ask," she said, hushed. "Are you a creature of the night? I mean, I've seen you during the day and you didn't burn up or glitter like diamonds in the sun, but there are those marks on Ulric's neck and—"

I laughed. It was the only thing I could do. "Right, don't I wish. Anyway, they're both wrong. I jumped. I saw my Dad's stupid PI poking around down in the bushes and went to chase him off."

"Gen, you could have been hurt!"

"Yeah, well, too late for second thoughts on that now. Sorry I woke you. Did the party go late?"

"Yeah, the cops closed us down just after you left. I guess one of your neighbors called them."

Wow, it must have gotten *really* rowdy for my neighbors to notice.

"Damn, I missed all the fun. Anything on for tomorrow night?"

"Why, have you heard anything?" she asked.

"Just hoping."

"I'll let you know," she answered, finishing on a yawn.

"You get some sleep," I ordered.

"'K."

I closed the phone and turned to Maya. "Nothing yet on the party plans, but my secret's still safe. More or less." And speaking of secrets... "Did you get anything out of the

Prickly Princess that might tell us where all this is going down?"

Maya and Sid exchanged a look. "She bit her own tongue off to keep from talking," Maya said. "She's more afraid of Rasputin than of us. We're still waiting for it to grow back."

"Gross!"

For the rest of the night, I was put to work helping with the site research.

•   •   •

The day kicked off with grief from Richardson in home-room for dragging my bodacious, black-clad butt in a few minutes late. I explained why I didn't have a note—the whole emancipated minor thing—but as far as he was concerned, if I was old enough to be on my own, I should be responsible enough to get to school on time. Only, what it took me a sentence to say, *he* turned into a lecture. I couldn't exactly counter that he should cut me some slack because facing down a Mad Monk took a lot out of a girl, so I had to put up with the whole thing.

In fact, I suffered through the entire day, straight up until eighth period, wondering if I'd been wrong. Maybe word wasn't going out. Maybe the Prickly Princess had caught me at the movie theater because she'd been there scoping it out for the release of their new gaseous formula. Or maybe...but as I was sitting in my final class contem-plating calling in my new theory, the cell phone I'd gotten to replace the one Alistaire stole vibrated. I surreptitiously slid the cell out of my pocket to peek at the message that had come in. *Bingo!* As good as her word, Lily had texted me the party plans. I'd just hit *forward* and sent the text on to Maya and Sid when the shadow of Mrs. Parker loomed over me, her hand out, demanding that I turn the phone over to her.

I did, as meek and mild as if I was totally not myself. The truth was, I was too busy thinking. I *knew* that address Lily had sent. In the hundreds that had come up last night, that had been one of them. It wasn't a numbered road, like Rt. 9, 52, 82—hike!—which meant it was probably residential rather than business, the home of one of the students. Not Gavin's, I knew, but beyond that—ack. I almost wished I could rifle through my own brain like the psycho-psychic to pull out the info. I wondered what he was up to. How long would it take him to finish with Raspy and come for us? A long, long time, I hoped.

Suddenly, I had it. It popped into my head with the clarity of a web page, which was exactly where I'd seen it. In my searches last night of online yellow and white pages, I'd found the home addresses of Raspy's new lackeys, our newly made vamps Tyler and Teresa. I didn't know if Teresa's parents had gone out of town, like mine had, to party down the pain of her death, or if they were intended to be victims as well, but we were partying at her place tonight.

I wondered what the others thought of that, or if they even realized it.

I sent Bobby a mental memo, and he sent back a *see you there.* I didn't hear anything else the rest of class, as I tried to figure out how we were going to stop Raspy's retinue, the council contingent, and their human helpers from releasing the gas. They all knew the plan and the lay of the land, and we didn't. At least with the Mad Monk himself out of the picture, Bobby's mesmerizing powers would be working at full force.

When the final bell rang, I dashed into the hallway, looking for the others in the explosion of students. Byron found me first. "You got the message?" he asked.

"Yeah, Lily sent the deets, thanks. Then Parker took my phone."

"Who you gonna call? We'll all be together."

"Great," I said, trying to inject enthusiasm into my voice. "Whose idea was this, anyway? Seems kind of sudden."

Byron grabbed my arm, put it through his, and started leading me toward the parking lot. "Do you need to stop at your locker first?"

"No, I'm good."

"Okay then. It was Bella's idea. Memorial for Tyler and Teresa."

"Trashing her parent's place?"

"Word is they've put it up for sale and gone out of town. Moved in with relatives or something. We're being respectful. Bella's going to take up a collection for funeral costs … you know, in case the bodies are ever recovered."

"You don't think that's a little weird?" I asked, wondering if Byron might be working with the vamps himself.

He shrugged. "Like there's such a thing as normal. The word is that Tyler and Teresa busted their way out of the morgue vaults. How crazy is that? And have you seen the bite marks on Ulric's neck? Nothing for it but to have a dead man's party."

I swallowed hard. Ulric. I was going to have to face him. I'd never confronted one of my, er, blood donors post-bite before. I had no idea if the same power that made them docile made them forget, or if they remembered every second of it. I so hoped for the former. I couldn't tell if the latter would have Ulric outing me as a bloodsucker or thinking the bite constituted second base and wanting to try for a home run. With Ulric, it could be anything.

"I'm all for a party," I said, realizing I had to say something.

"Cool."

We were the first to the hearse, but Lily and Gavin appeared about three seconds later, arm in arm. Finally, Ulric and Bella showed up. The latter wouldn't meet my eyes at all, which was just as well, because I didn't have a clue what to say to her after what she'd done to me. I only knew what I *wanted* to say to her, but not in front of the others. It was more a gesture, anyway, involving my foot and her ass.

Ulric, though … As I was afraid they would, his eyes glowed like he thought he might get an encore on the necking tonight.

"Hey," he said. He managed to toss a whole conversation into the word, something like *I know. You know I know. I know you know I know, and I'm willing to keep the secret but I want more.* I was going to have to do something about him. The question was, what?

"Gen and I are going together," he continued, surprising the heck out of me. "We'll take her car. I need to stop for party supplies."

Now Bella looked from me to Ulric, suspicion narrowing her eyes.

"That *all* you want to do?" Lily teased, either missing the undertones or trying to lighten things up.

"As a matter of fact, no," Ulric answered, a wolfish grin spreading across his face as he put an arm around my shoulders. He gave me a squeeze that was a little more than friendly, as if to let me know I'd better go along if I didn't want a scene.

I responded with a pinch to his butt that was also a little more than friendly. Everyone but Bella laughed when he jumped.

"Don't be long," Bella said, locking eyes with me. I wondered just what they'd planned and worried for a second that whatever Ulric intended would make me late for it, but surely it wouldn't. Based on the party at Red Rock, more and more people would arrive as the evening went on. The vamps wouldn't want to play to a half-full house. Besides, they didn't have our sunscreen additive ... yet, anyway ... so they couldn't start until dark. Even if Rick really had gone over to the dark side, he had no more idea than Bobby and I did as to what was added to our bottled blood. Even if the vamps had gotten a sample, they'd have to reverse engineer the stuff. They couldn't possibly have had the time.

"Come on," said Ulric, steering me toward my car. "We really do have a stop to make."

"Where?" I asked, echoing Bella's suspicion.

"The hospital. I don't care who ordered us out. You're getting up to see Bram and you're going to save him."

We hit my car, one row over, and I ordered him in. As soon as the doors were shut, insulating us from the outside world, I turned on him.

"I want to help Bram. I do. But…" What could I say that wouldn't confirm Ulric's…well, "suspicions" would probably be understating the matter. Denial was out. "I don't know what a transfusion might do to him, without us doing the whole blood exchange."

"So exchange. He's dying or as good as dead anyway in that coma. Do you think he's going to argue?"

I'd never really needed the vamp power of mesmerism. Bobby was an exceptionally special case, being able to control multiple targets and move things with his mind, so early in his unlife. As I understood it, powers generally grew with age, and not nearly so great as Bobby's. I was only a few months old in vamp time, so my hypnotic powers were sketchy at best, but I poured all the sincerity and strength I could muster into my next words and hoped it would be enough for Ulric to go along. I could overpower him, but leaving him helpless and behind with vamps like Alistaire running around town seemed a little over-the-top.

"Ulric, when all of this is over, I promise to do what I can for Bram, but you have to trust me when I say that right now, we have to get to that party."

"Something's going on, isn't it? Bella—"

"Yes. In fact, it's safer for you if you don't go. If I can drop you somewhere—"

"Hell with that! Why didn't you warn the others?" He reached for his phone, and I had to put my hand over his to stop him.

"We can't. Bella's one of them. You've guessed that already. If we tip her off, if I chase everyone down and blow the party, they'll just do it some other time and place when we're not ready for them."

"And you're ready for them now? You? All by your lonesome?"

"Yes, me. And no, not alone. That's all you need to know."

"Bullshit. These are *my friends*."

"Mine too, dammit."

He was silent for a second, as if I'd surprised him.

"Well ... all right then. What's the plan?"

"No clue. Give me a second."

I put the car into gear and started to pull out, gritting my teeth as I paused to keep from running over the throngs walking behind me, unaware that cars might be about to back into them. Logically, I knew that nothing could begin yet, at least on the vampire end of things, but sometime in the few hours between now and nightfall someone would be releasing Raspy's new and improved formula into the air, creating a whole house party of highly suggestible teens. No telling where that might lead, if someone got suicidal or aggressive or—

I gunned the car to hurry the next sauntering pair along and hit the road as fast as I could. Ulric had a death grip on the dash until I suggested that the seat belt might be a lot more useful. Then I called Bobby.

Hey, stud, I said mentally.

Yo, babe.

Yo? Since when do you "yo"?

Um, trying it out.

I was not going to point out that Bobby was *so* not street. I suppose he was pretty fly for a white guy.

What's the plan? I said instead.

Maya and Sid already have eyes on the place. Other than that, we're essentially on our own until evening when the vamps and the Feds' strike team arrive. They're staying away until then so the vamps don't catch a whiff of the trap before we close in.

So we just hang tight until night?

We keep an eye on the collaborators and find some way to stop the release of the gas, or neutralize it without tipping them off.

Wow, is that all?

In a nutshell.

Can't you just, you know, magic them into not *releasing the gas?* I asked.

The vamps may be waiting on some kind of signal before moving in, Bobby told me. *We don't know what it is, so again…*

We can't risk it, I finished for him. *Okay, fine. I'll watch Bella, but you've got Rick.*

I understood that we had to let the council and Grunge Vamp go ahead and spring their trap, but caution and I weren't exactly best buds. In fact, caution and I were more like plaid and polka dots, two things that just didn't go together.

"Turn here," Ulric ordered.

Who's there with you? Bobby asked.

I looked at Ulric. *I'm, uh, kinda bringing my own back-up.*

Gina! It was loaded with that frustration I usually heard from teachers. *What part of undercover don't you understand?*

You know, I told him, *I put cloth covers on my textbooks, too, but it doesn't mean anyone mistakes them for throw pillows.*

Huh? What on earth does that mean?

Ta!

I tuned him out by focusing on Ulric. "Okay, here's the plan. I'm keeping an eye on Bella. I want you to circulate. Keep a watch on everyone else. Make sure no one is acting strangely. Well, more strangely than usual. If someone's hurt or there's any kind of trouble, you see what it's all about. I'm not going to come running unless I know it's legit, in case it's a diversion."

"Gotcha, but—"

"You want to help, you do what I say."

"It's not that. What if Bella's ready for you, like she was the other night? At least, I thought that's what I saw. I was a little, uh, dreamy."

"I'm ready for *her* this time. Just in case, you get to keep an eye on everybody plus me." I wasn't going to mention

Bobby and blow his cover any more than it already was, just in case Ulric got mind-controlled or something crazy like that.

"This is Teresa's road," Ulric said, pointing off to the left.

It was hardly more than a gravel path. More like a long driveway than a street. Only a few drives led off of it, either to one-story homes on small lots or bigger homes mostly hidden behind trees. Some of the drives were paved, but most, like Teresa's, were dirt. I nearly left the underside of my Nissan behind in a rut. The drive curved up a hillside, ending at a wood-shingled one-story house, well away from its neighbors and isolated by tall pines.

No wonder our villainous vamps had chosen it. The place was perfect. Only one rutted road out. No one would be making a quick getaway, even if they could easily get their cars out of the knot already forming on the lawn.

The only wrong note about the place was that it had a decent amount of windows. Releasing a gas there didn't make any sense. We could just open the windows or break the glass or—but maybe it was like mustard gas or tear gas or something like that, strong enough to work even with ventilation. It was a scary thought.

I parked alongside the driveway far from the other cars. If my parking brake didn't give out and send my car rolling down the hill without me, I ought to be able to get out quickly to give chase, or evacuate if need be. Bobby would be so proud of me for thinking ahead.

I was about to call and tell him when I spotted the hearse.

"The others are already here," I said, proving I'd totally mastered the obvious, even if I'd completely blown the whole secret-identity thing.

"Guess we'd better get going."

Ulric reached into his shirt and pulled out a big honkin' cross of antiqued silver, flared stylistically at the ends. I recoiled, and it was all I could do not to hiss, which would be so cliché.

He gave me one of his shit-eating grins. "Don't worry. If you decide you want a repeat of the other night, I'll take it off for you."

"In your dreams, Goth Boy."

"Absolutely," he answered.

I tried not to smile, but I couldn't help myself. My teeth even peaked a little bit at the thought of a second helping of him. But then I remembered Bobby. Sweet, sexy, good kisser. All that *and* a bag of chips. Everyone always used that expression. It was one thing when the chips were lamo potato, completely another when they were chocolate. Anyway...

"Let's go," I said, getting out of the car. I left my door unlocked, for a quick getaway. Ulric followed my lead.

The door to Teresa's place was slightly ajar, music leaking out, so all we had to do was push our way through. Inside, what I could see that wasn't already covered in partiers was woodsman chic, if that wasn't a total oxymoron. The furniture was made all of planks and rough-cut logs; the couch was covered in what looked like finely woven burlap. In the center of the room was an area rug that had—I had to look twice—moose and bears in fields of earth tones. Miraculously, there were no deer heads mounted anywhere ... that I could see, anyway. I looked around for Bella but found Rick-the-rat first, chatting up some blond bimbo. Not that I had a problem with blonds—seriously—but there was *no way* they had more fun.

Ah, there she was. The living room looked right into the kitchen through a breakfast bar topped with something like slate. It smelled as though someone had spent the day baking apple pies, but with the family gone that didn't seem terribly likely. I was betting it was some kind of plug-in or air freshener, like I probably should have put up in my place.

I didn't want to get too close to Bella in case, like Ulric had said, she had a surprise waiting for me, but I watched her like a hawk. Only she wasn't doing anything at all interesting, just standing beside a doorway in the kitchen that looked like it should have led to a pantry but apparently didn't. Not the way she seemed to be talking to someone through the doorway before she turned and yelled, "Hey, Gavin says there's a pool table downstairs!"

The exodus didn't start immediately, but in ones and twos and threes, people eventually migrated to the basement, where there were only two very tiny windows way up high and only one other door out. I was totally not thrilled with the defensive possibilities, though it was hard to get a truly sinister sense of a place that smelled like apple pie. If anything, the scent was even stronger down in the basement, probably to cover the smell of mold or mildew or all those other basementy things.

Bobby had arrived a while ago with a small gaggle of geeks—it was totally a gaggle of geeks, a nest of nerds, a dollop of dweebs. My eye had been instantly drawn to him when he'd entered, but I quickly sneered and looked away for Ulric's benefit. Speaking of Ulric, I steered him over to the one other door out of the basement and tested it. Locked. Of course. I twisted the little button in the knob to unlock it and still it wouldn't budge. So not a good sign. Not at all. If anything happened, if we had a stampede or something, kids would get run over or bottlenecked at the top of the stairs. The place was a death trap.

Worse, as the afternoon turned into evening, more and more people crowded into the basement to keep the noise and lights in this supposedly uninhabited house from alerting the neighbors, who might call the police.

I relayed all the info I had to Bobby who, I was pretty sure, had picked up on it himself and was passing it along to Agents Stick and Stuffed via telepathy or whatever. Ulric left my side to circulate, as he had a few times already, grabbing himself a beer along the way, but this time the light coming through the two small windows was starting to dim. It was getting near show time, and I was as jumpy as a swimsuit model about to take her first runway walk.

He brought back a brew for me as well.

"You know I can't drink this, right?" I asked him softly.

"Relax. I'm not trying to get you drunk. It's camou-flage, in case anyone notices you've been going empty-handed. Besides, a broken beer bottle makes a pretty good weapon in a pinch."

"I'm not even going to ask how you know that."

"Good. I'd tell you, but then I'd have to kill you."

I gave him a sidelong look and his lips twitched.

"Bella's making a move," he said, nodding in the direction from which he'd come.

Bella was headed for the stairs to the first floor. Rick, coming from the other end of the room, wasn't far behind her.

You see? Bobby asked in my head.

Yup.

On it, he said.

Me too.

We converged on them, and when Ulric started to fol-low, I stopped him with a talk-to-the-hand sort of gesture. "I need you to stay behind. If something goes wrong, if you hear the hiss of gas escaping or smell anything at all, I want you to beat down the doors. Break the little win-dows. Keep everyone calm and get them out if you can. If you can't, focus them. Get them singing Beyoncé or Kanye or, hell, Taylor Swift. Something to tune out the rest of the world. Got me?"

He didn't look like he liked the thought of being kept out of the action, but he didn't argue.

"Ulric, promise me," I said, just to be sure he wasn't

silently plotting. "And don't wait until you're sure about the gas. If you even think you hear it, make a move. Okay?"

"Do I get a reward?" he asked hopefully.

"Yeah, maybe you get to live."

He made a face at me and leaned in for a quick, hard kiss I was totally unprepared for.

I pushed him back, but his wolfish grin was already in place. "For luck," he said.

I hit him, but maybe not as hard as I should have, and raced up the stairs after Bobby, only to hear a lock click into place before we could get through.

"Can you whammy it?" I asked Bobby, close behind him.

He closed his eyes and reached a hand out to the knob, as if he could see through the tips of his fingers.

I heard the lock click back out of alignment and Bobby gave the knob a twist, but the door didn't budge. Just like the one downstairs, the door had been jammed shut.

"On three," Bobby said.

We both backed down a step, prepared to launch full out for the door.

"One. Two. Three."

We flew forward, bashing our shoulders into it to no effect.

"Hey, what's going on?" someone asked from below. "You're blocking the door."

"It's jammed," Bobby answered.

"Duh," someone else said. "Let me try."

The voice sounded vaguely familiar. I turned to look, and my heart sunk into my stomach like the deadweight it was. The voice belonged to Rick's pal, the redheaded sweatchild from the hospital bathroom. If he recognized me, which seemed pretty likely since I was still totally in goth regalia, things could get ugly, especially if he had any of the vamps' previous potion left in his system.

"Bobby," I said softly. "Powers again?"

"I'm working on it, but whatever they've wedged the door shut with is in good."

"Sure," I said to Red, nearly choking on my sweetness. "You try it. You're probably a lot stronger than me."

He preened like a peacock and strutted up the stairs, which was not nearly as easy as it sounds. No wonder he was a jock, with coordination like that.

I stepped aside, pressing myself against the wall to allow Red to take his aggressions out on the door. Maybe it would save us some trouble down the line.

Bobby's eyes met mine, and I felt another blast of power leave him, blow through the door, and slam something against a far wall. Whatever had been jamming the door shut?

Red took the nod Bobby gave me as a cue to take his turn on the door. He started a step down, hand on the knob so he could turn it and ram the door at the same time. He almost fell through it, which made Bobby and me look like weenies, but, hey, it worked.

"Bring a bunch of beer back down with you," one of his friends called. "We're getting low."

But I wasn't sure Red was going to get the chance. Rick stood in the kitchen, staring fixedly at us. I couldn't tell a thing from his expression. Bella was nowhere in sight, but neither was the sun. The door had delayed us just long enough for full dark to fall. We were out of time.

17

Quick, where's Bella?" Bobby asked. "We have to stop this before it goes any further."

Rick raised his gaze to the guy behind us—Red.

"Will you do the honors?" he asked.

Red stepped more fully into the kitchen and closed the door behind him. He locked it while Bobby and I stared, stunned stupid.

"What?" Rick asked, an evil grin from ear to ear. "You

thought I was on your side? Please. The only thing you've ever gotten me is trouble—and a crappy government job."

I still didn't know if it was Rick or some kind of mind-control speaking, but I saw Red. Literally. He reached for the wedge to jam the door shut again, and I wasn't going to let that happen.

I flew into action, launching myself at Red as Bobby went for Rick. One good kick sent the wedge somersaulting across the kitchen. Red whirled toward the counter, looking for the knife block that was next to the stove. I was too fast for him and got there first. I didn't really need a blade to do damage, but I knew from experience that some guys wouldn't take a girl seriously unless she had a weapon, especially when he topped her by nearly a foot.

I pulled out the blade with the biggest handle, and it was a nasty-looking thing—very sharp and pointy, blade as smooth as glass.

Red's eyes went super-sized. "Where's Bella?" I asked, holding the knife hip height for me, which put it right about level with his twig and berries. He winced.

"Where are you releasing the gas?" I continued, giving the point of the knife an experimental twitch in threat. I didn't turn to look at the thrashing off to the side. I trusted Bobby to handle Rick-the-rat.

Sweat popped out on Red's brow and his face began to live up to his nickname. "You can't stop it. It's already done."

"What? I don't smell anything." And with my super-vamp senses, you'd think I would.

"No? Apples and cinnamon?"

"It's in the air freshener!" Crap on a cracker. We were too late. Now that I knew, it made total sense. There hadn't been any outbreaks of violence of any kind at this party—it seemed like the perfected formula made the peeps not just suggestible, but docile. The psycho-psychic had it right. Rasputin and Company were aiming for sheep.

Lily, Gavin, Byron...I only hoped Ulric had enough of himself left, even under the influence, to lead them to safety.

"Where's Bella?" I demanded again.

I heard a crash in the basement and realized we'd been had. While Red and Rick kept us busy upstairs, the vile vamps had come in through the other basement door.

I felt Bobby send forth a blast of power, but it seemed to blow back on us, nearly rolling my eyes back in their sockets.

"It's not possible!" Bobby gasped, releasing Rick's collar and letting him slump to the floor.

"What?" I asked, afraid I already knew.

"I've only felt that once before. *Rasputin.* If my power's blown, it can only mean he's back."

Heck with the cracker—the crap was totally hitting the fan. Raspy had slipped Alistaire's grip, and it seemed Rick had truly gone over to the dark side. We had no defense. They'd know we were Feds, know we'd have back-up, which, come to think of it, they'd already taken out once, back at the morgue. We couldn't count on Sid and Maya to have our backs. And without them to call in the strike team...I just had to hope there was some fallback in place.

Red made a move while I was distracted, and instinctively I flashed out with the knife. His blood spurted like a geyser and he fell against the beautiful breakfast bar, holding his innards, well, *in*.

"You cut me," he said in disbelief.

"You're shocked by this?"

Bobby delivered a boot to Rick's head, which put him over the edge into oblivion so he couldn't do any more damage. "Let's go!" Bobby said.

"You circle the house and sneak in behind them, through the other basement door. I've got this one."

Bobby nodded and was off like a shot.

For once, I curbed my impulse to fly into action and forced myself to *think*. Plotting didn't exactly come naturally to me, but fear was a great motivator. Raspy alone was way more powerful than me. Apparently, more powerful even than *Alistaire*. And he had minions of both the fanged and the fresh-blooded variety. An entire houseful, if I didn't get a move on.

It came to me in a flash. Actually, Bella'd given me the idea, poisoning me with garlic. What better place to find garlic than a kitchen. Turn about was totally fair play. I blew through the place like a tornado, opening doors and drawers until I found what I was looking for—plastic sandwich bags, garlic powder, and cooking oil. I used two of the baggies on my hands so I wouldn't burn myself, poured oil into the other bags, then divided the garlic powder among them. I shook them up for good measure. Garlic bombs. Hopefully enough to save us.

I tucked the bags into my shirt and dashed for the door downstairs. It opened onto eerie quiet. No party sounds. No laughter or shrieks or scuffling. I could only see a bit of the room from the top of the stairs—the backs of people's heads. Someone had their attention. Their total, exclusive attention.

"Come, *milaya*, join us," Raspy's accented voice called up to me. There was power behind it. Force. I could feel it the way I could feel Bobby's, but all it did was wash over me, dimpling my skin.

Still, I descended a few stairs, the better to see the big picture. Kids were frozen, seemingly in whatever position Raspy's retinue had caught them in. Among them walked two vamps I didn't recognize, but they had that arrogant air of council.

I looked beyond them to the other door, where Raspy and his entourage stood just inside, Bella-the-betrayer behind them.

As I watched, Rasputin said, quietly but with power, "Come," indicating with a curl of his fingers the front line of kids, Ulric among them. Ulric stepped forward just as readily as the others. Teresa, Tyler, Grunge, and Raspy each grabbed one of the waiting victims and bit down on their necks.

The advantage of garlic bombs over gunfire was that I didn't have to worry about collateral damage. Any humans hit would be stinky, but no more. I pulled the first two bags out of my shirt and launched them at Raspy and Grunge. I hit Teresa and some random kid, but there was enough splatter that two out of the four villain vamps raised fangs to hiss at me.

The council vamps, however, were closing in. "Freeze!" one ordered. Apparently, he hadn't gotten the memo on my full mental measure of ornery.

Needless to say, I didn't freeze. Two more garlic grenades were already incoming. Both hit the mouthy one dead center of the chest—either luck was with me or my aim was getting better. Loud Mouth screamed and flailed at his clothes like he was on fire. The nearest kids seemed to shrink away fractionally, as if the commotion was breaking through their programming. But not enough to free them. Not really.

The vamp I'd hit had his shirt off now, flung down at his feet. Even though his chest still smoked, he was coming at me. But I had another two baggies in hand. There were only about four more in my shirt—at this rate, I was going to run out of ammunition before I ran out of targets. I needed a back-up plan.

I launched the two bags I had in hand, one at each of the onrushing council vamps. One went wide, but the other stopped Loud Mouth's friend just long enough for me to whip my head around looking for a new weapon. But I was stuck on a staircase... a *wooden* staircase.

I threw myself on the railing, trying to rip it out of the wall as Loud Mouth reached me and went for my knees, taking them out from under me. I kept hold of the wooden rail and it came down with me. All of it. Not just handy stake-sized fragments. I used it as a club to beat the side of the baddy's head.

From across the room came a second crash, like the rail coming down, only different. I looked up to see the door behind Raspy being busted in. By Bobby...and he had back-up. I gave a whoop of triumph, which ended in a howl of pain.

In my distraction, someone had stabbed deep into my thigh. I looked down into the feral face of council vamp number two—he'd uprooted one of the uprights left behind when I'd ripped out the rail and impaled me with it. It was a good thing his partner was still lying half across my stomach and chest, concussed from my bludgeoning, or I'd have been a goner. The stake would have been aimed at something a lot more vital.

But even as I thought this, searing pain tunneled my vision. My hands tightened convulsively on my wooden club and I swung it toward the vamp, putting all the pain and outrage I felt into the blow. I knocked him to the ground, and I tried to throw his partner off me, but it was no good. I'd used up the last of my strength.

All I could do was sit and watch as Bobby grabbed Raspy and thrust him away from his victim. Raspy thrashed at Bobby with his teeth, but Bobby nearly punched them out. I was so proud I could almost burst...until Raspy recovered and his gaze met Bobby's. Bobby went as still as death, and fear stabbed me at least as hard as the stupid council vamp.

The strike team was busy with Teresa, Tyler, and Grunge, trusting Bobby to take care of Raspy. They didn't immediately notice the change.

"Attack!" Rasputin ordered him. Bobby didn't have my

resistance to mesmerism—he was either about to do something he'd never forgive himself for, like kill his own strike-team members, or go down himself. I couldn't let it happen.

Rasputin turned his gaze back to the rest of the kids, who were shifting, restless, but hadn't yet broken free of his control. "All of you, attack the newcomers!" he ordered.

As one, the kids converged on the strike team.

Crap on a crispy, crumbly cracker.

One more time I tried, summoning up all the strength I could. For Bobby. For Ulric and Lily and all the others. I went for the stake this time, hoping that if I could pull the wood from my body, my strength would return.

Grunting with the huge effort, I yanked. The stake slid free with a sound I hoped never to hear again, a wet tearing sound, almost like the time I'd had to wrestle with a pool filter over my bikini top, only much, much worse.

Strength didn't exactly return in force, but my vision expanded once again so that I could see *exactly* how much trouble we were in. The kids... and Bobby... overwhelmed the strike team, which had disappeared beneath their onslaught. Raspy was coming right at me.

I pushed the council creep off my lap, and he rolled down the stairs. Raspy took them two at a time, vaulting his downed comrade to clutch my neck with his crazy, claw-like hands. I didn't need to breathe, but his nails were piercing my skin. If he hit my jugular or whatever... if I lost my remaining blood... he could probably rip my head clean off before I could summon the strength to fight back. It was now or never.

I brought my knee up in the move every girl knows from the age of five, maybe earlier. Just like any other man, Raspy winced. He lost a little height as he curled around his battered bits, but he didn't let go of me. In fact, his eyes flared blood red in the way I'd seen Alistaire's do when he was feeling especially psychotic.

I didn't want to have to do it, but he gave me no choice. There was nothing left but the foolproof grab and twist. And I *really* didn't want to grab.

Steeling myself much like I had with the stake, I went for him, grabbed his tortured testes in my hand and squeezed. His eyes went supernova, but his control was inhuman. Instead of just releasing me, he flung me across the room. A couple of bodies broke my fall and lay there looking dazed, like I'd knocked the sense out of them ... or maybe back in.

Raspy leapt down after me, and I momentarily thought about trying to turn the army to me, but that would mean using them as human cannon fodder. Raspy wouldn't hesitate to go through them to get to me. But what if I could turn them from attack to stampede?

It was worth a try. I took a mega breath, filling my lungs to full capacity and focusing all the power I might possibly have, and shouted at the top of my voice, "Out, now! Everybody, upstairs. *This* way!"

I bolted for the stairway. Right at Raspy. I might get trampled, but at least I wouldn't be alone. I didn't have a millisecond to spare to look behind me before I was clashing again with the Mad Monk. "Mad" didn't even do him justice. He was furious, his eyes practically burning holes through mine, drilling into my head.

Then I was jostled from behind. Then pushed, my feet actually skidding forward toward the stairs. Raspy's feet got tangled with mine and we both went down, me falling on top of him like an inhuman shield as the kids trampled over us, stampeding more like cattle than sheep, crushing my vertebrae.

For a minute or more all I knew was pain, and when it finally ended, I couldn't have moved if I'd been goosed. But the kids were up and out of danger. At least—

· · ·

A pair of hands grabbed me by the shoulders and I didn't even have enough left in me to panic. Gently, they turned me over, cuddling me into a body. I blinked slowly to clear the haze from my eyes and met Bobby's baby blues.

I had to wet my mouth to speak. "You're alive," I said. It wasn't much more than a breath, really, hardly an actual sound.

"In a manner of speaking anyway. Are you okay?" He stroked the hair away from my face, so, so gently.

I coughed, and it *killed*. "I think my back is broken." But I didn't want to dwell on that or the worry that it was too much to heal and that I might come out looking like the Hunchback of Notre Dame. I looked around, but my head didn't want to turn. Just my eyes moved. Rasputin was still right there, a hand's breath from me, only my hands weren't working. He wasn't moving, which was really strange, since my body should have sheltered him from the worst.

"Is he … faking?" I asked Bobby.

He shifted minutely, as careful as possible not to hurt me as he reached for Raspy, but still, I heard bones grind together in my back and a wave of nausea washed over me. He poked the Mad Monk, and his body rocked just enough to give us a glimpse of the stake I'd yanked from my leg and thrust aside—it was now buried in Raspy's back. What were the odds? Poetic justice that I'd actually beaten him with his own weapons. Byron would like that.

"Leave me here," I ordered Bobby. "Lock down the baddies, see to the others. I'm not going anywhere."

"You need blood."

"After," I said. My eyes wanted to close, but I didn't dare let them until Bobby did what I said. Otherwise, I was afraid he wouldn't leave my side.

I waited until he gently laid me back on the floor and pressed a kiss to my forehead. "I'll be right back."

He got those crappy zip-tie cuffs off the fallen strike team, and I passed out in relief.

18

It was really, really short-lived relief. Pain shocked me awake. Someone was trying to twist me like taffy.

My eyes shot open and I stared into the dark brown eyes of a man in face paint—the stealth kind of paint, I guessed, because it sure didn't do a thing for him otherwise.

"I've got you," Bobby said. I turned to look into his much nicer baby blues, which, weirdly, glistened with a single red tear on the verge of spilling over. "Just squeeze my hand when it hurts. Blade says he's got to straighten you out or you'll heal wrong."

Like Alistaire healed, I thought, just as—Blade?—gave another twist and all I could think of was *Holy Freakin' Mother of God make it STOP!*

When I could speak again, I sought out those brown eyes. "I hate you," I said.

"I can live with that," Blade answered. He had almost a bluesy voice, the kind that sounded like it was just about to give out. Rough, like a hundred miles of bad road, and low like low-rise jeans. If he hadn't just tortured me, it might have given me a little thrill.

Blade, as good as his name, pulled out a knife, did a little flip thing with his wrist to free the blade and cut himself where the sleeve of his shirt had been pulled back above his gloves.

"Here," he said, holding his welling wrist to my mouth, "drink this, you'll heal faster. An ambulance has been called for people bitten by the bleeders...er, other vampires...and those run over in the stampede."

"But everyone will be okay, right?" I asked, my eyes riveted on that blood. Raspy and I had been the only ones in the way of the rushing kids. Hopefully we'd gotten the worst of it.

"Blood loss, maybe some concussions and broken ribs, legs...mostly from my team fighting back when the kids were ordered to attack us. But we were as careful as we could be. They'll heal."

I'd almost forgotten what my question was as I watched

his blood, dripping, some of it already lost. Like the mind, a terrible thing to waste. I licked my lips, and he helped me raise my head enough to drink.

Bobby looked away.

The blood—warm and wonderful—flowed into my mouth, and I sucked greedily. I could almost feel my insides knitting themselves together. Strength was returning, and I was beginning to feel almost normal again when Blade pulled away.

He checked his watch, black like the rest of his outfit. "We're out of time. Estimated EMT response to this site is ten minutes. We've already burned five. We've got to get the gang out of here before the police arrive, or before the EMTs show up to look for a pulse."

"Do you need help?" Bobby asked.

"You just take care of the girl. Get her on her feet. You two are going to have to stay here to spin the tale. New drug on the market... hallucinations... kids thinking they're vampires... mass hysteria." He shrugged, "It's worked before."

Bobby gave him a nod and turned back to me. Already I felt like even if I couldn't leap buildings in a single bound, at least I could enter them under my own steam. I tried to sit up, but Bobby wouldn't let me.

"Not yet. Give it time."

I gave him a sour face, but did as he said.

"Sid and Maya?" I asked.

"Vamps drained them, but not to death. Some nice bloody steak and a few days' rest, and they'll be good as new. They managed to round up the kids as they stormed out."

"So we won?" I asked.

"We did."

I smiled, and Bobby smiled back. For a really awesome moment, the room, the strike team and their walking wounded, ceased to exist. Bobby's gaze held a promise of what was to come later...much later, when my back was all healed and I'd bathed, showered, spritzed, and moisturized. It was a shame I had to ruin the moment...for now, anyway.

"You think you can handle spinning the tale on your own?"

He blinked, and his smile faded away. "Yeah, but why?"

"I have a promise to keep."

"Can't it wait?"

"I'm not sure it can." Who was I to say how much time Bram had? Or how much time *I* had before Maya and Sid whisked us away to another mission. I might even have to sneak out all stealthy-like.

"You need back-up?" he asked.

"Nope, I'm good. Besides, we've got everyone."

"Except Alistaire."

"Assuming Raspy left him alive."

"Just be careful. I'll be listening for you."

I creaked as I stood up, like an old lady, but at least everything was working. Bobby didn't look at me like I was an old lady, though, and I stepped into his arms before I left, tilted his head to just the right angle and pressed my lips to his. I had to stand on tiptoes to do it, but he was worth it. Bobby's lips were firm and wonderful. They opened under mine, and his tongue slipped out to tease me. My heart wanted to start just so it could pound, but I broke away before the police and paramedics could arrive and mess with my plans.

"That's only a taste," I teased.

"Good."

I took the stairs two at a time and left the house the way I'd come in. The lawn was a confusion of kids, still under the influence of the gas but now following Sid and Maya's lead. Both of them looked shaky and as drained as I knew them to be, but they were tough. They were holding their own.

I stayed as far away from them as possible and kept to the shadows. They'd hear my car starting up, but there was nothing I could do about that. I doubted they were up for a high-speed chase, even if they wanted that kind of attention.

I'd paid attention coming in, and once I hit a main road, I knew my way to the hospital. Once there, I knew the way to Bram's room. I just had to wait for the reception lady to be distracted and take the elevators up.

It was after visiting hours, but I was lucky. At this time of night there was only a skeleton crew on, with the expectation that most of the patients would be sleeping or, in Bram's case, even further indisposed.

The nurse's station was deserted as I came off the elevator, and I slipped into Bram's room without incident.

There he was—machines beeping and booping. He looked smaller than when I'd last seen him, like he'd sunk into the bed. His perfect head seemed sound, and I wanted to stroke it, to see those dark chocolate eyes with those ridiculously long lashes open. And there was only one way short of a miracle to manage that.

I thought about blood...Ulric's, actually, since I could still remember the rush of it. No thin stream like Blade had offered me, but a raging river. My teeth descended, and I nicked myself in the wrist. I used my other hand to open Bram's mouth. It was heartbreakingly easy—his muscles offered no resistance at all. I dripped my blood into his open mouth, enough to fill a small juice glass. I didn't want him to drown in it, but I was afraid that was exactly what would happen. He wasn't swallowing, and if he breathed it in...I tried something I'd seen once on some animal show with people fostering baby animals. I closed his mouth and stroked his throat to encourage him to swallow.

"Come on, come on, come on," I said under my breath.

Beneath my hand, his Adam's apple bobbed, and I let my breath out in a sigh of relief. He'd taken the blood. Now it was a waiting game to see how he'd respond.

My wrist was already healing so I didn't need to wrap it, which was good, because even though this was a hospital, they didn't exactly have gauze lying around like tissues. I spotted a chair deep in the shadows of the room, lit only by a faint light in the headboard of the bed, and settled in to watch.

I nearly jumped out of my skin when the door to the room opened and closed. I had to will myself to stay still, hoping the nurse coming to take his pulse or whatever didn't notice me there.

I wasn't prepared for Ulric and the others.

"I knew you couldn't stay away," Ulric said, but his smirk was tired; his heart wasn't in it.

"That's right," I answered. "It's all about you."

"Oh sure," Lily said. "Give him a swelled head and then leave us." She looked away. "That's what you're going to do, isn't it?"

"How did you—? Why aren't you with the others?" I asked.

"Ulric snapped out of the trance or whatever before anyone else," Gavin supplied.

"Maybe because of your warning," Ulric said, his dark eyes all intense in the low light.

"Or maybe because of his hard head," Gavin cut in. "Anyway, he got to us too, once we were out of that house, and explained on the way over...more or less. Now here we are."

"I knew you'd come," Ulric said.

"How is he?" Byron asked.

We all looked at Bram, and I swore I saw his eyelids flutter. And then...no doubt about it, his hand twitched.

Lily ran to his bed and I wanted to do the same, but if he was waking up, the machines would alert the staff pretty soon and we'd have company.

"We'd all better get out of here," I said, surprised to hear my voice crack just a bit. "It's after hours, and someone's going to come by to check on him in just a bit. You don't want to get caught."

"We're not leaving," Lily said, steel in her voice. "We're going to be right here when he wakes up."

"He won't be—?" Gavin started and stopped, unwilling to finish.

I looked back at Bram, and at Lily stroking his cheek. "I've never done this before. I don't know if he'll have a sensitivity to sunlight for a while, or any weird cravings, but no, he won't be…like me."

"Thank you," Ulric said. "For…everything."

Bram's beautiful eyes opened slowly, and I so wanted to stay. I'd never gotten the chance to know him, and I already knew the others enough to miss them. They all were instantly at his bedside. As much as I wanted to be there too, my place was elsewhere. I slunk silently to the door, wary of good-byes, and had nearly closed it behind me before it was caught.

I turned. Ulric held the door in his hand, staring at me with his heart shining in his eyes. "We ever going to see you again?" he asked, trying to sound casual.

"You never know," I answered.

And I disappeared into the night. Another name, another mission. At least I'd always have Bobby…or else. Even the Feds weren't ready for the diva-storm I would unleash if they ever tried to keep *us* apart.

The End.

Acknowledgments

There are so many people I want to thank that I don't even know where to start. I absolutely couldn't do this without my fabulous agent, Kristin Nelson, and everyone else at the Nelson Literary Agency, including Sarah Megibow, Lindsay Mergens, and Anita Mumm. I also want to thank the incredible people at Flux: my editors Brian Farrey and Sandy Sullivan, my publicist Marissa Pederson, copywriter Courtney Huber, and amazing cover designer Lisa Novak.

On the personal side, I want to thank my awesome family, who I love very much and who put up with my main character practically living among us; Lynn Flewelling, who looked over an early draft when I had no idea if I was recapping too much or not enough; my cheerleader Beth Dunne and her very cool family; the Girlfriends' Cyber Circuit, because they're an amazing group of girls, some of whom started and all of whom have gotten behind the YA Authors Against Bullying movement. Thanks to Guy DuQuesnay, for being one of the first people to listen to me go on and on with an overlong recitation of the plot of my very first, very terrible manuscript and for pimping me in his newsletter, and to Milo Kaciak, who listened as well and would, I'm sure, pimp my books if he had a newsletter. (Right, Milo? Just agree with me, it's easier.)

I also want to thank my unbelievable authors, who've been super and supportive, and every reviewer, blogger, or fan who's ever had a kind word to say. I appreciate you more than you know.